There was another crackling sound. No, it wasn't crackling. It was short and raspy. Like a bike chain switching gears. Chain! That's what it was. The light chains. Someone was tugging them off one by one. And whoever it was was getting closer to the storage room.

"Hello," I called out. There was no reply.

"Uncle Stoppard?" I heard another chain being pulled. The light outside the storage room door was growing dimmer.

I stood up from where I had been sitting on the floor. Why didn't I stay up in the apartment like Uncle Stoppard asked me? Why did he have to go to that stupid library and read about some stupid pygmies?

Footsteps echoed in the basement. Someone was trying to be quiet, but I could hear them walking closer to the storage room. I tiptoed closer to the door. Very gently I placed a hand on the door. I was going to push it open farther.

The door pushed back.

It swung shut and trapped me inside the room. I heard a scraping sound. The padlock was being snapped shut.

I leaned against the door, but it was shut tight.

I was locked inside. Just like the man on the floor with the rat tur~~ and the blue legs. The horizontal man.

THE
HORIZONTAL
M ◆ A ◆ N

A FINNEGAN ZWAKE MYSTERY

MICHAEL DAHL

AN ARCHWAY PAPERBACK
Published by POCKET BOOKS
New York London Toronto Sydney Tokyo Singapore

AN ARCHWAY PAPERBACK *Original*

An Archway Paperback published by
POCKET BOOKS, a division of Simon & Schuster Inc.
1230 Avenue of the Americas, New York, NY 10020

ISBN: 0-671-03269-0

First Archway Paperback printing August 1999

10 9 8 7 6 5 4 3 2 1

AN ARCHWAY PAPERBACK and colophon are
registered trademarks of Simon & Schuster Inc.

Front cover illustration by Lisa Falkenstern

Printed in the U.S.A.

IL 7+

To Danny
for everything

THE
HORIZONTAL
M · A · N

1

The Horizontal Man

Before I saw the dead body, I used to like raisins.

In fact, I used to love raisins: raisin toast, raisin muffins, raisin pudding, raisin cereal. Now I look at one of those dried-up grapes, and all I see is a dried-out corpse. This morning at the breakfast table Uncle Stoppard set a plate in front of me with two giant raisin muffins, steaming with melted butter. I must have had a funny look on my face, because right away Uncle Stoppard asked what was wrong.

"You promise you won't laugh?" I asked.

"Promise," he said.

So I told him. His cucumber-green eyes got squinty: it was his serious look. "But, Finnegan," he said. "And I don't mean to say it sounds weird," he said. "But, why on earth should raisins remind you of that dead body we found in the—" Uncle Stoppard stopped. He stared down at the muffin on his own plate. Then he stared at me. Then he stared at the muffin again.

"Because of the . . . rodents?" he said quietly.

"Yeah," I said. "The . . . rodents."

Uncle Stoppard's complexion began to match the color of his eyes. He pushed himself away from the table, scooped up our plates, and scraped all four muffins into the waste can.

"How do you feel about waffles?" he said.

I don't know why I felt that sick. I mean, yes, it was the first dead body I ever saw. But I should have been more comfortable. After all, my whole family loves dead things.

One of my grandmothers, for instance, was a paleontologist and collected fossils for museums. My grandfather worked in the Dead Letter department of the Tombstone, Arizona, post office. Aunt Verona became a taxidermist after she got out of the Army, and used to display all her preserved pets in mock battle scenes on her front lawn. Uncle Stoppard says her neighbors called the place "The WAC's Museum." Dad's favorite band is the Grateful Dead. Mom's favorite writer is Robert Graves. Both my parents were archeologists. I mean, *are* archeologists. I mean, *both.* Both are both. As of this moment they're alive, but considered legally dead, since they disappeared over seven years ago while searching for Tquuli the Haunted City somewhere among the frozen volcano-cones of Iceland. (It was written up in *Peephole* magazine.) How do I know they're alive? I just know.

I'm staying with Uncle Stoppard until my parents come back. To look at us, you'd never guess we were related. Uncle Stoppard is tall and muscular with wavy red hair, crinkly green eyes, and a big nose (he calls it *aquiline*). I am not tall or muscular, have light-brown hair, pale skin, and freckles. Uncle Stoppard says I have a *moccachino* crop, *java* eyes, and a *triple-latte* complexion with *nutmeg sprinkles.* Uncle Stoppard likes drinking coffee. He also likes using unusual words.

The only thing we share is our glasses. I mean, we both *wear* glasses. And, of course, we share the family fondness for dead things: I like ghost stories and Uncle Stop spends most of his time plotting to kill people. We've been living together a little more than seven years now, and I guess I've gotten used to living in his apartment in Minneapolis. I don't think about my parents as much as I used to. Now I only think about them a couple times a day.

Poor Uncle Stoppard. Maybe I shouldn't have mentioned the raisins at breakfast.

Last year, Uncle Stoppard had a hard time eating because of fingerprints. He was reading all about fingerprints in these crime books of his and he learned what they're made of. Sweat. I mean, fingerprints are made of sweat, not the crime books. And sweat is full of stuff like ammonia, phosphate, uric acid, and cholesterol. Yummy, huh? Did you know that one of the fatty acids that oozes out of your pores is the same stuff that crayons are made from? Each time Uncle Stoppard picked up a pear or a sandwich, he thought about how those sweat chemicals got all over the food he was planning to eat. He thought about that a lot. Last year, he lost twelve pounds.

"That's all right," he used to say. "It's good for my diet."

Uncle Stoppard doesn't need to diet. He rides his bike and blades and lifts weights. He looks like one of those guys in the jeans commercials on TV. When he's not exercising, Uncle Stop writes murder mysteries. That's what I meant when I said he's always plotting to kill people.

His last mystery, *Cold Feet,* has been on the New York Times bestseller list for eight weeks. That's as good as Stephen King. *Cold Feet* is about this killer who always leaves a pair of blue shoes next to the dead bodies of his victims. Lots of readers think it's funny to send Uncle Stop a pair of blue shoes through the mail. We have bags and bags of fan letters and packages stacked in our living room. In three weeks we've given away 200 pairs of blue shoes to the Salvation Army. Uncle Stop says it's a good arrangement since the Salvation Army likes saving soles.

Anyway, we found the dead body a week ago. I was still eating raisins at the time. It was the middle of June, on a gray and gloomy Sunday. I was helping Uncle Stoppard go through the mail. We have a system. First we put all the packages in one pile and all the envelopes in another. Then we divide the packages into two categories: Probably Shoes and Probably Not. The Probably Not packages are weird shapes that a shoe wouldn't be able to fit into. Some fans send presents like food, or homemade socks, or pencil holders, or pictures of themselves and their families. Some send typed pages of mystery stories they've written, hoping that Uncle Stoppard will get them published. Uncle Stoppard says he still has trouble publishing his own books.

I was about to rip open a large, flat package that looked like it contained another manuscript when I glanced at the address again. The name on the address was not Uncle Stoppard's. It said: Pablo DeSoto. We live in south Minneapolis near Lake Calhoun. Our building is made out of dusty yellow bricks (Uncle Stoppard calls them "marigold"), with green shutters ("emerald"), and a steep, slanty roof ("alpine"). It has two apartments on the very top, two in the middle, and one sort of half underground. The laundry room and storage rooms fill in the rest of the basement. Uncle Stop's and my apartment (no. 2) is in the middle level. Pablo (no. 3) is our neighbor across the hall landing. I figured that somehow Pablo's package got mixed up with ours in the hall. This happens about two or three times a week. Since we get so much mail, the caretaker puts our packages on our landing, next to our door, which is next to Pablo's door. And sometimes packages for Pablo get stuck with ours.

I ran down the hall stairs to the mail slots in the front entryway. The slots were too narrow for Pablo's package. Not wanting to leave it sitting on the floor, I ran back up the stairs to our landing and knocked on number 3. No answer. I went back inside our apartment and decided I'd try again later. I set the package just inside our door.

It was cold and windy outside, so I stayed in the rest of the day. By lunchtime, we still hadn't opened up all the mail. I counted twenty-two more pairs of shoes, including a pair of turquoise high heels and some indigo sneakers. Uncle Stoppard went back to his office and typed on his computer. I went to my bedroom and read comic books. This was supposed to be summer vacation. Where's the sun? The only bright spot in the whole apartment was the picture I kept on my dresser.

The picture is a color photograph of me and my parents. It was taken a month before they left for

Iceland. My parents, Anna and Leo Zwake, were in Agualar, near Mexico, on an archeological expedition for the world-famous Ackerberg Institute. They were searching for an ancient Mayan city in the jungle. I was only a five-year-old kid, but they took me along with them. The photo was taken on a bright, summery day. We must have been having a picnic, because my parents are sitting on a blanket with plates and cups scattered around. I am sitting on my mother's lap. We are all smiling and squinting in the hot sun. It's the only picture I have of my family.

Funny, but I actually have memories of that day. I can remember the heat of my mother's pale yellow dress when she set me on her lap. I remember the thunder of my father's laugh. A nearby river murmured softly. Birds. Women's voices.

In the picture I am sitting next to a shiny figurine. It is one of the Mayan artifacts that my parents discovered on the trip. Once they unbury an object, clean it off, record it, videotape it, figure out what it is, and stare at it for a few days, they pack it up and ship it off to the Ackerberg guys in Washington, D.C. The figurine in the photo, the one I'm grabbing with my five-year-old paws, is a man sleeping on his side. He's made out of gold.

The small statue is called the Horizontal Man. I know this, not from memory, but from the notation on the back of the photograph. Written by hand, it says: "Anna and Leo Finnegan. With the Horizontal Man. Agualar." Agualar is a country near Mexico. I know, because I looked it up in an atlas.

Why didn't my parents take me to Iceland? Was I

that much trouble in Agualar? I don't look like trouble in the picture. We all look happy.

Next to the photo, lying flat on top of my dresser, is something else my parents left with me: a Mayan gold coin. It's not really a coin because Mayan people didn't use money to buy things, they used chocolate. If a Mayan boy wanted to buy a new pair of sneakers, he would hand the shopkeeper a bag of cocoa beans. I call it a coin because it's round like a half-dollar and flat as a dime. And it's pure gold. It probably fell off some royal Mayan guy's costume. At least that's what I think from digging through a lot of history books at the library.

Later that afternoon I was still in my room when I heard footsteps on the front stairs. I thought it must be Pablo. I grabbed the package next to the door and stepped into the hall. Pablo's front door was open. I walked into his apartment. Pablo wasn't there.

"What do you want?" said an angry voice.

I spun around and saw a dark shadow. It was Ms. Pryce, the caretaker, standing in the doorway of Pablo's kitchen.

"You're not supposed to be in here," she said.

Uncle Stoppard says that Ms. Pryce has a monochromatic wardrobe. That means she dresses in only one color: black. At this moment, Ms. Pryce was wearing a black sweater, tight black pants, black socks, and black shoes. She had black lipstick and shiny black fingernails. Her spiky hair is shorter than Uncle Stop's. And much brighter. Ms. Pryce has hair the color of a summer sky. I wonder what color the sky is in Iceland?

Ms. Pryce was scratching her blue hair when she asked me again, "Why are you here?"

"This package," I said. I held it up like a shield in front of me. "It's Pablo's. I, uh, we got it by mistake."

"Just set it down someplace," she said. "And then leave. You shouldn't be in other people's apartments." I looked for a good place to put the package, someplace Pablo would see it right away.

"You don't see paper anywhere, do you?" asked Ms. Pryce. She pushed past me and stomped through the room. "I have to leave a message for Mr. DeSoto. Some people don't pay their rent on time," she said. "Some people are two weeks late. Oh, great, he didn't even bolt the back door. That's real smart."

I noticed a pad and pencil on a table next to the door. "There's some paper," I said.

She walked past me again and grabbed the pad.

"And some people get too much mail," she said. Ms. Pryce was busily scribbling a note on the pad, her spiky blue head bent down. She wasn't looking at me, but I knew she meant me and Uncle Stoppard when she made that comment about the mail. It wasn't our fault, we didn't ask for all that footwear.

That gave me an idea. Ms. Pryce obviously liked at least one other color besides black.

"Um, what's your shoe size?" I asked.

Ms. Pryce stared at me as if I were some unfamiliar and disgusting creature.

"Chew? Did you say chew?" she said.

"Shoe," I said. "But, never mind."

I was going to put Pablo's package down on the small table by the door, when Ms. Pryce said, "Leave Mr. DeSoto's mail in there." She pointed to the living room. Then she placed the pad back on the small table. "I want my message to be the first thing he sees when he gets back from that conference of his."

The living room had lots of tall, leafy plants and a big-screen TV. A fancy glass coffee table was covered with shiny magazines.

Something else sat on the table. Actually, it *slept* on the table. A small golden figurine of a man. The Horizontal Man.

The small golden man lay on his side with his head turned. He had round, staring eyes, thick eyebrows, a spiral navel, and he wore sandals and a loincloth made of feathers. A tiny knife hung on a belt. All of it was gold. Even his toes.

And there he was, sitting on the coffee table in Pablo's living room.

I ran across the hall, through our front door and into my bedroom. I stared at the photo of me and my parents. I grabbed a magnifying glass from my desk drawer and studied the tiny Horizontal Man in the picture. It was the same statue. It gleamed the same dull, yellow color.

I sat down on my bed, breathing hard. It felt as if I had just run around the block twenty times. What was the Horizontal Man doing in Pablo DeSoto's apartment? I ran back through the apartment and across the hall. Pablo's door was shut. I knocked but there was no answer. Ms. Pryce must have gone back to her apartment. Maybe she'd let me back in to take another look. I ran down the stairs to her apartment. She had her name stenciled on a purple card tacked to the center of the door: V. Pryce.

What was I going to say to her? What reason could I give her to let me inside Pablo's place? Ms. Pryce had very definite ideas about people being in other people's apartments. Maybe if I said he had stolen something from my uncle.

Luckily, I didn't have to lie. Unluckily, she didn't answer the door when I rang her bell. She must have gone out.

I ran back upstairs to our apartment and stood outside Uncle Stoppard's office. I hated to disturb him, but this couldn't wait.

I opened the door and saw Uncle Stoppard staring at his computer screen.

"Finn, haven't I told you—" said Uncle Stoppard.

"Sorry, Uncle Stoppard."

"You look like you've been running a marathon, Finn. What's wrong? Are you sick?"

I nodded. "Sort of. It's on Pablo's coffee table," I said.

"You threw up on Pablo's coffee table?"

"The Horizontal Man."

"You threw up on a horizontal man?"

"No. He's on the table."

"There's a horizontal man lying on Pablo's coffee table?"

"Yes, with the same feathers and loincloth and eyebrows and everything," I said.

Uncle Stoppard raised one of his eyebrows. "I hope you didn't disturb Pablo while he was entertaining guests."

"No, but—"

"Haven't I always told you to knock first?"

"Yes, but—"

"Speaking of which, you didn't knock before you came in here, either."

"But Ms. Pryce was already over there," I said.

"With the horizontal man?" asked Uncle Stoppard. I nodded.

Uncle Stoppard tapped a pencil against his cheek. "I find it rather odd," he said, "that Pablo would throw a party this early in the day. I find it especially odd that he would invite Ms. Pryce."

"It wasn't a party," I said. "It was *this*." I handed him the photo.

"Your parents?"

"That statue is the Horizontal Man," I pointed out. "And that same statue is in Pablo's living room. On his coffee table."

"And Ms Pryce . . . ?"

I explained what Ms. Pryce was doing, and why I was over in Mr. DeSoto's apartment in the first place.

"Finn, how could Pablo possibly have this same statue?"

"I don't know, but he does."

"It's probably a replica."

"A what?" I said.

"Replica," he said. "When people go to museums and see statues they like, they can buy copies, or replicas, in the gift shop on the way out."

"Are replicas made of gold?" I asked.

"Not usually." Uncle Stoppard jumped up from his chair. "Oh, no!"

"What?" I said.

"The museum," he groaned.

"What museum?"

"Any museum," he said. Uncle Stoppard flopped

back down and gave me that squinty look. His serious look.

"I am so stupid," said Uncle Stoppard. "I don't believe how thoughtless I can be. Finn, you are living with an imbecile. A loon. And I don't mean the state bird." He took a deep breath. "The statue in Pablo's living room—"

"The Horizontal Man," I said.

"Yes, the Horizontal Man," he said. "It may not be a replica."

"Right."

"It may be the real thing."

"That's what I said."

"We have to establish our facts first, Finn. We don't want to just go ahead and accuse someone of stealing."

"You think Pablo stole it, too, huh?"

"I don't see any other explanation," said Uncle Stoppard.

"But where did he get it?" I asked.

"From downstairs."

"Downstairs?"

"That's where I kept your parents' stuff," said Uncle Stoppard. "In the basement."

There's a store in the Mall of America that Uncle Stoppard and I have visited a few times. It sells all kinds of optical illusions. They have these round spinners with spiral lines drawn on them. You spin them like tops, and if you stare at them long enough, you feel like you're getting hypnotized. That's how I felt now. Hypnotized. Unreal. Uncle Stoppard's office spun around me. My parents' things were locked up in a room in the basement? Why didn't Uncle Stoppard tell me before?

"I didn't tell you before," said Uncle Stoppard. "Because you were so young. And, quite honestly, Finn, I forgot. I am so dumb. That stuff has been down there for over seven years."

Uncle Stoppard explained that my parents had left Agualar in a rush. A huge hurricane in the Gulf of Mexico, which had been heading toward Texas, suddenly changed its course. Agualar was hit with hundred-mile-an-hour winds and a wave surge thirty feet high. My folks and their crew quickly crated up all the important artifacts, abandoned their tents to the blows of Hurricane Midge, and flew back to Minneapolis and Uncle Stoppard's apartment, bringing their golden discoveries with them. I guess my folks didn't have a regular house in those days. Anyway, my parents were snapped up by the Ackerberg Institute to work on another expedition in Iceland. They had to leave the very next day from Uncle Stoppard's apartment. So, they handed Uncle Stop their stuff from the Agualar trip (and me) and then zoomed away to the North Atlantic.

"Why didn't they take me?" I asked.

"They were afraid the extreme temperature change might be bad for you. You were just a little kid. Going from the tropical jungle to the frozen north might be unhealthy."

"But I like snow," I said. Which is a good thing if you live in Minnesota.

"Anna asked me to keep the stuff they found in Agualar and ship it off to the Iceberg Institute."

"Ackerberg," I said.

"Yeah. I have the address written down some-where."

Uncle Stoppard's office looks like an explosion in a paper factory. He'd be lucky to find that address in another seven years. "Maybe I should look it up on the Net," he said.

"So there's gold locked up in the basement?" I asked.

"Not so loud!"

"Sorry."

"I didn't know it was gold," he whispered. "And then I forgot about it. I had other things on my mind at the time. My books and—" Uncle Stoppard looked down at his sneakers.

"And me," I said.

"Lots of things," he said. "But I wasn't worried about anyone taking it. No one else knows it's down there."

"Except maybe the Ackerberg guys," I suggested.

"I wonder why they never contacted me," said Uncle Stoppard.

I looked at the mountain ranges of notebooks, mag-azines, books, and unopened mail that bordered the walls of his office. A letter might lie there, like a Mayan artifact, undiscovered for centuries.

"The gold is safe," said Uncle Stoppard. "It's all boxed up."

The treasures of Agualar were right under Uncle Stoppard's aquiline nose. Under my own bedroom floor.

"I guess that talk about replicas and museums re-minded me," said Uncle Stoppard. He stood up from his chair a second time—slower this time—and put his hand on my shoulder.

"Come here, Finn." He led me into the kitchen by the back stairway. He reached up, and took a small key that hung on a nail by the back door. Then he leaned over and handed it to me.

"This is the key to the storeroom," he said. "I haven't been down there in a while, but all the storage doors are numbered with the same numbers as the apartments. Go on down, and I'll be right with you. I have to shut off the computer."

A string of lightbulbs led to the back of the basement. You had to pull on a separate chain to turn each one on. And each time I pulled a chain, another part of the basement lit up. It was cool and quiet down there. The storage rooms were way in the back. Past the washing machines and dryers, past the big cleaning tubs and drains, past the switchboxes on the wall and the locked-up bicycles that belonged to the two nurses who lived up on the top floor.

Along a narrow hallway, were the storage rooms. Uncle Stoppard was half right about the numbers. There were numbers on the doors, all right. But not just one number. Two. Each storage room was shared by two different apartments. I stopped at the one that had "Apts. 2–3" painted on it.

That could explain how Pablo had the Horizontal Man. If it was the same statue that my parents dug up in Agualar, and had been locked inside here, Pablo could have seen it one day and decided to take it.

I wondered what other golden treasures from Mexico were buried inside, as I fitted the key into the

shiny lock. It didn't turn. The key Uncle Stoppard gave me was the wrong key.

A funny noise came from inside the storage room. It was like the sound you make when you crunch up paper. Or when you burn waffles. Burn? Maybe there was a fire inside the storage room.

I hurried down the gloomy narrow hall and ran right into Uncle Stoppard's belt buckle.

"Now where are you going?" he asked.

"Waffles!" I said. "I mean, burning waffles. I mean, fire!"

"Fire . . . ? I don't smell any smoke."

Uncle Stoppard was right. There was no smoke in the air. But there was another, unpleasant aroma.

"Smells like old cheese down here," said Uncle Stoppard, wrinkling his nose. Ugh. Very old cheese.

"And this is the wrong key," I said.

He took it from my hand. "It's the right key."

He fitted the key into the padlock and tried turning it. It didn't work for him, either.

"See?" I said. "It's the wrong key."

"No," he said. "It's the wrong lock. Look at this padlock."

The lock was bright silver. There was a thick black band around the bottom with the brand name stamped on it. Nothing could bust through that lock. "Looks good and strong," I said.

"And brand new. The lock that used to be here was old, just like this key."

The key was dull and smudged, like a dirty nickel. I glanced at the other locks on the other doors in that gray hallway. Only our padlock stood out, gleaming like a shiny, new dime.

"Someone changed the lock on us." Uncle Stoppard swore and punched the door with his fist. We heard the crinkling, scratching sound grow louder.

Uncle Stoppard looked at me, his green eyes as big as grapes. "Something's inside."

"Fire?"

He shook his head.

"Thieves," I said.

"Finn, how could thieves padlock the door behind themselves?" Good question. I guess that's why Uncle Stoppard writes mystery books. He darted to a work-bench in a corner of the basement and returned with a screwdriver and a hammer. "I read about this in one of my crime books," he said.

Uncle Stoppard placed the head of the screwdriver against the pin in the upper door hinge. He pounded with the hammer. In less than a minute, he removed both pins from the upper and lower hinges.

"Now all we have to do," he said, "is pull the door out like this and—"

He stopped. The cheesy smell zinged my nose hairs.

"Finn," he said quietly. "Maybe you should go back upstairs. You shouldn't see this."

Too late. I already saw it. The body of a man sprawled on his stomach on the floor of the storage room. The body wore khaki shorts, and I could see that the legs were a creepy, blue color. All around the body were tiny, dark, dried-up blobs. Rat turds.

They looked like raisins.

2
Fingerprints

Ms. Pryce threw up in one of the big tubs in the basement. Mr. Barrymore threw up in the back hallway. He lives in apartment number 5 on the top floor across the hall from the two nurses, Miss Brazil and Miss Bellini. Miss Brazil and Miss Bellini did not throw up. They're probably used to seeing dead bodies. This was my very first dead body, but I did not get sick. Not even when I heard the reason why the raisin turds were all over the dead guy's body. I heard one of the police officers say to another one, "Well, I suppose mice gotta eat, just like everybody else." Then his buddy said, "You mean, rats, don'tcha?" My stomach got tight and started flopping around, but at least I didn't lose my lunch.

After Uncle Stoppard and I had discovered the body, we rushed back to the apartment and called 911. Then Uncle Stoppard ran down to Ms. Pryce's apartment and told her. She started screaming. In a few minutes, I heard more screaming outside. I thought Ms. Pryce had flipped out and was running around on the lawn. The noise came from three white police cars and an ambulance. Uncle Stoppard took the detectives and the police officers into the basement. One of the detectives was a black woman named Detective Linker. She was dressed like a regular person, not a police officer. She wore a blue jacket, a white shirt, and dark pants. Her thick, black hair was tied in a ponytail, and she even wore tiny gold earrings. Detectives wear earrings? When I looked closer I noticed the earrings were actually tiny handcuffs. When we all reached the basement, that's when we found Ms. Pryce throwing up in one of the washtubs.

"I hope you haven't disturbed any evidence, ma'am," said Detective Linker.

"No," said Ms. Pryce. "But the evidence sure disturbed me."

Detective Linker and the man detective drew pictures of the body and made a map of the basement. I sat on the stairs and watched them. They prowled all over the room looking for clues. They even crawled on the floor, and sniffed the tubs (even the one Ms. Pryce threw up in). At the tub, Detective Linker said, "Looks like blood, Bryan."

Bryan, the other detective, examined the tub and poked at something with a pencil. He looked at Ms. Pryce and said, "This blood isn't yours, is it?"

"Certainly not," said Ms. Pryce. Then she ran over and threw up in the other tub. "Perhaps you should go upstairs, ma'am," said Bryan.

Ms. Pryce, her face as white as tuna in a can, shuffled up the stairs while the detectives investigated the rest of the room. They stared at the walls and the stairs and the plumbing. When they finished, Bryan said to Detective Linker, "I guess we better let the uniforms in." That's what they call the regular police officers. Uniforms.

Four uniforms with incredibly shiny shoes walked in and consulted with Bryan and Detective Linker. After two of the uniforms marched back upstairs, Detective Linker questioned me and Uncle Stoppard first, since we had discovered the dead guy. Uncle Stoppard explained what happened.

"But why did you break into the storage room?" Detective Linker asked.

"It's my storage room," said Uncle Stoppard. "I didn't break in."

"I'd call using a hammer and screwdriver breaking in," she said. "Why didn't you use your key?"

"It didn't fit," he said.

"Your own key didn't fit into your own storage room?"

"It's a new padlock," said Uncle Stoppard. "Someone put a new lock on it."

"When was the last time you were in that room?" asked the detective.

"I'm not sure. Maybe a few weeks ago."

"And your key worked then?"

"Yes."

"Why did you come down this afternoon?" she asked.

"We were looking for some things that belong to my nephew, Finn," said Uncle Stoppard.

"Things that were stolen," I said.

The detective looked at me for the first time. "Stolen?"

"I think so," I said.

"Finn," said Uncle Stoppard. "We'll talk about that later."

"Okay," I said. Then I turned to the detective. "It's our neighbor. Pablo DeSoto."

Uncle Stoppard groaned. "Finn, we don't know that for sure."

"And what did he steal?" asked the detective.

"A statue that belonged to my parents. They're archeologists."

"How do you know Mr. DeSoto stole it?"

I told Detective Linker about the Horizontal Man and she jotted everything down in her notebook. Then she walked over to the police—uh, uniforms—who were examining the storage room door and padlock. "What have we found?" she asked them.

A young police officer with a yellow mustache and sideburns turned to her. "Two sets of fingerprints. One big, one small. Small one probably belongs to the kid."

Detective Linker walked back to us. "We'll need to get your fingerprints, Mr. Sterling."

"You've already got them," he said.

"Oh, really?"

"I worked as a teller in a bank once. So my fingerprints should be on file."

"We'd still like to make our own copies," she said. "If you don't mind."

Why didn't she ask for *my* fingerprints?

"Do me a favor," said Detective Linker. She stepped into the storage room and stood over the blue-legged body without looking at it. (That takes practice.) "Can you tell if anything is missing in here?" she asked.

Uncle Stoppard and I stood by the door and peeked in. By this time, I couldn't smell the cheesy odor anymore. I must be getting used to it.

"There was a set of luggage over there." Uncle Stoppard pointed. I could see rectangles in the dust where the suitcases must have been sitting. "And I think some boxes were taken off those shelves."

"That's good," said Detective Linker. "If you notice anything later, let us know."

"When can we go back in that room?" I asked.

"Tomorrow morning. We'll be taking some pictures tonight and checking a few things. Oh, and one more thing," she said to Uncle Stoppard. "You're certain you don't know who the body belongs to?"

"Sorry," said Uncle Stoppard. "It doesn't look familiar. Of course, it's hard to tell without much of a face left."

The detective rubbed her nose and looked at me. "Where does this Mr. DeSoto live?"

"Across the hall," I said.

"Apartment number three," said Uncle Stoppard.

"But he's not in town," I said. "He's away for business."

"Is he?" said the detective. She looked like she thought I was lying. "We'll check on that, too." She strolled over to Bryan, who was examining one of the basement windows.

The young policeman with the yellow mustache finished his work on the storage door. He picked up his fingerprint kit and set it on top of one of the washing machines.

"Hey, you're Stoppard Sterling," he said.

Uncle Stoppard nodded.

"I really got a kick out of your *Cold Feet*. It was great."

"Thanks," said Uncle Stoppard.

"I like the stuff you put in the book about fingerprints."

"I hope I got all my facts straight."

"You sure did," said the officer. "Lot of mysteries are full of baloney, things that could never happen. But I like the science stuff." He reached into his shirt pocket. "Here's my card," he said.

Uncle Stoppard read it, and then I looked at it. Jared Lemon-Olsen.

"Lemon-Olsen?" I said.

"Yeah, it's a combo of my parents' last names," said Jared. "If you ever do more research on fingerprints, Mr. Sterling, let me know. I got tons of books on the subject, and a couple years of experience." Then he grinned. "I could give you some Lemon aid."

I thought only Uncle Stoppard made jokes like that.

"Did you get some prints off the lock?" asked Uncle Stoppard.

"Yeah. Two sets. Probably yours and the kid's. We also found some on the door frame that we're gonna check. Maybe some will turn up on the body."

"You can get fingerprints from skin?" I asked.

Jared nodded. "If we get them fast enough. In a cool basement like this, prints on a body might last a couple of days. You'd be surprised where we find fingerprints."

"What about mine?" I asked.

"What about yours?"

"Are you gonna take mine?" I said.

"Yup, we have to take everyone's."

He pulled out a white card from his kit. It was covered with blue lines and divided into little squares. Then he pulled out an ink pad and set it on top of one of the machines.

"Just relax." Jared grabbed my right hand. "I'll do all the work." He pushed my fingers, one by one, into the squishy ink pad. Then he carefully rolled each finger across one of the squares on the white card. He did the same thing with my left hand.

"I thought my right hand had the same fingerprints as my left hand," I said. "Just in reverse."

Jared laughed. I noticed that he had a smudge of black ink on his yellow mustache. "Nope," he said. "Each finger is different. There, you'll want to wash that off."

I ran my hands under cold water in one of the tubs, and dried them against my shorts.

It was Uncle Stoppard's turn to get inked. Two big guys from the ambulance tromped down the stairs with a stretcher, covered the body in plastic, and then disappeared up the stairs with it. They acted like it was no big deal, like they were carrying groceries.

Bryan shouted up at them, "Just leave it in the hall for a while. Don't take it out 'til everyone's IDed it."

Uncle Stoppard asked Jared, "Can we go back upstairs?"

"Sure, if we have any more questions, we'll let you know."

"How do you guys get rid of the smell?" asked Uncle Stoppard.

"Nasty, ain't it?" said Jared. "I never get used to it. Just take a shower and it should be okay. By the way, you like salsa?"

"I do," I said.

"Good. Eat a little before you go to bed. It'll help knock the smell out of your sinuses."

"Cool," I said.

Our apartment seemed quiet after all the noise and people in the basement. After we both showered, Uncle Stoppard pulled a jar of salsa out of the refrigerator. We sat at the kitchen table and dipped crackers into the jar.

"I'll bet it was Mr. DeSoto," I said.

"The dead body?" said Uncle Stoppard.

"No, the killer," I said. "He's the only other person with a key to the storage room."

"Our key didn't work, remember," said Uncle Stoppard. "It was a different lock."

"Oh, yeah," I said. "I'll bet it was Ms. Pryce."

We could hear the uniforms walking up and down the stairs in the back hallway. Poor Mr. Barrymore. When they brought him down from his apartment to identify the body, he threw up. Mr. Barrymore had just come home from some Scottish festival and was wearing a kilt. The kilt had purple and green and orange squares. Uncle Stoppard calls those "Munchkin colors." Mr. Barrymore looked miserable (I could tell because I was peeking through the blinds in our kitchen window). I can't think of anything more embarrassing than throwing up in front of strangers while wearing a kilt.

Uncle Stoppard yawned and turned away from the window. "I'm sure the police will figure all this out."

"Why don't you solve the murder," I said.

Uncle Stoppard smiled sleepily. "I'm not a detective, Finn."

"But you know how to kill people in books."

"Those are books."

"And you know how to figure out clues," I said.

"I can figure out the clues because I'm the one who put them there in the first place," said Uncle Stoppard. "I already know who the killer is."

"Yeah, but *how* do you know who the killer is?" I asked.

"I create the killer. And I work with an outline before I even write the story. That's how I know it all fits together."

"So? Work it out like an outline. Pretend this is before the story starts."

"Before the story starts, huh?" Uncle Stoppard yawned a second time. "I think we better both go to bed." He looked at his wristwatch. "Jeez, it's already eleven o'clock. And I have to go to the library in the morning."

I was surprised how tired I was. You'd think I'd be more excited. It's not everyday you find a dead body in the basement. Or learn that buried treasure is hiding right beneath your feet. I planned to go back to the storage room tomorrow and rummage through my parents' stuff. Maybe there would be more pictures to look at. More treasure to donate to museums.

Uncle Stoppard was snoring as I passed his bedroom on the way to my own room. I slipped into my pajamas, slid under the covers, and turned off the light. I could hear Mr. Barrymore and the two nurses climbing up the creaking stairs to their apartments. The police were laughing outside my window. Car doors slammed. Engines revved up and then disappeared into the distance.

I must have fallen asleep. The next thing I remember was hearing footsteps again. Slow, tired footsteps, trudging up the back steps. The steps sounded too heavy for Ms. Pryce. I got up and looked at the timer on the microwave in the kitchen. The glowing numbers showed 5:02. Almost dawn.

I tiptoed across the cold kitchen tiles and placed my ear next to the back door. The steps grew louder. They reached our landing and then stopped. I heard the jingling of keys. Quietly, I lifted one of the blinds on the back window.

The two hallways in our building are nothing like each other. The front hall is a spooky, narrow stairway with thick, blood-red carpeting. As the carpet spirals up toward the roof, it passes by each apartment's front door. The back hallway is wide and full of windows. It's more like three long, separate landings connected by three separate staircases. Each landing has two doors, the back doors to the apartments on that level. And next to each door is the kitchen window for that apartment. When Miss Brazil and Miss Bellini come home, they always use the back stairs: they climb up to our second-floor landing, walk past Pablo's door, across the full length of the landing, past our back door, and then climb the next set of steps up to the third floor.

Whenever anyone enters the back hallway, the lights on each landing turn on automatically. The lights are supposed to frighten away thieves. This time they didn't do their job. Peering through our kitchen window, and into the lighted second-floor landing, I could see the back of a man in a dark gray suit carrying a suitcase and a plastic bag over his shoulder. It was Pablo DeSoto. Pablo the Thief.

I tiptoed back to my room, changed into a T-shirt and shorts, and let myself out the kitchen door into the back hall. Normally, I would feel afraid to knock on someone's door this early in the morning. But I didn't feel afraid. I felt mad. I rang the buzzer to Pablo's apartment.

A few seconds later, Pablo opened the door. He had taken off his jacket and shoes, but still had on a white business shirt and tie, and his gray pants. His dark hair was not combed as neatly as usual. His eyes looked red and wrinkly.

"Finnegan," he said. "Is something wrong?"

Now I felt scared. What was I doing over here?

"Where's your uncle?" he asked.

"Um, he's sleeping," I said. "But we found a dead body in the basement."

All the wrinkles disappeared from Pablo's eyes. "A dead body?"

"In your storage room. Well, our storage room. The one we share."

Pablo walked past me rapidly, then raced down the back steps. When I reached the basement, I found him switching on lights. The storage room door had been replaced on its hinges by the police, but the door was open. A bright yellow ribbon of police tape covered the entrance.

"It sure stinks down here," said Pablo.

"Ms. Pryce threw up in that tub," I said. "And the other one."

"Pryce was down here?" he asked.

"Everyone was down here. The police took pictures and asked everyone questions and took my fingerprints. They'll probably want to talk to you, too."

"I wasn't supposed to get back 'til tomorrow," Pablo said. "I took an earlier flight. I'll call them in the morning."

"Where did you go?" I asked.

"Seattle," said Pablo. "A computer convention. So who's the dead guy?"

"Nobody knows."

"Anyone see him hanging around here before?"

"They couldn't tell. His face was chewed off."

Pablo looked like he might add some airline food to the overused wash tubs. "Chewed off?"

"Rodents," I said. "The police said that even mice and rats gotta eat."

Pablo chuckled a little at that. Then he looked sick again. "So, how did this guy get in here, anyway?"

"Nobody knows that either," I said. "I think he was a thief."

Pablo poked his head into the storage room. "Is anything missing?" He spun around and stepped quickly away. "It smells worse in there. I need some water." Pablo walked over to a tub, and stuck his head under one of the faucets. Then he quickly pulled his head up. "This tub smells even worse. I gotta get out of here."

I turned off the lights and followed him back up to his apartment.

With all the running up and down the stairs, from my warm bedroom to the cool basement and back again, I must have been experiencing lots of temperature changes today. I still say my parents should have taken me with them to Iceland.

Pablo was sitting in his living room, his legs propped up on the glass coffee table, a glass of water in his hand.

"This is unreal," said Pablo, shaking his head. "A dead guy in the basement. And nobody knows who he is."

The night was getting stranger and stranger. I thought maybe I really wasn't in Pablo's apartment. Maybe this was just a nightmare. I looked at the glass coffee table. There were the plants. There were the shiny, new magazines. There was the package I had left for Pablo. And there were Pablo's stocking feet. The Horizontal Man, however, was gone.

"Where's—?" I started.

"Where's what?" asked Pablo.

"Um, your statue."

"Statue?"

"Didn't you have a gold statue on your table?"

"Gold?" Pablo took a gulp of water. "You've never been in here before, have you?"

"No," I said. "Well, just a little."

"A little?"

"I, uh, Uncle Stoppard accidentally got some of your mail, so I dropped it off in here. That's it there."

He picked up the package from the table. He gave it a funny look. "I thought my doors were locked."

"Ms. Pryce came in here to leave you a message."

"Pryce," he muttered. "That busybody."

"I asked her if I could leave this for you. It's too big to fit in the mailbox."

Pablo turned the package over and examined it. "So where did you find this?"

"With our mail," I said. "It got mixed up with all the stuff that Uncle Stoppard gets."

"My friend Larry was supposed to pick up all my mail for me. *And* water the plants. These African violets look terrible. Boy, you can't count on anyone these days." Pablo stood up and went into the kitchen. "Who does that Pryce think she is?" He grabbed a cold beer from the refrigerator and a watering can from under the sink. He wandered through his apartment, drinking from one can and watering the plants from the other. He must have had a hundred of them. Plants, I mean. "Oh jeez, and here's my rent check."

"Ms. Pryce mentioned something about the rent, too," I said.

"I hate it when she comes in here," Pablo said. "She's always coming in and leaving stupid messages." He was watering some purple flowery things in his dining room. "She probably takes things, too, for all I know. You said you saw a statue in here?"

"On your coffee table," I said.

"You're sure you didn't imagine it?"

"It was there all right."

"A golden statue?"

"Gold."

"And you saw it today?"

"Ask Ms. Pryce. She must have seen it, too."

"Yeah, I'll ask her all right. I'll ask her to stay out of my place. Maybe I'll change the locks without telling her." Pablo looked at me. "That reminds me. Tell your uncle I want to talk to him. When does he get home?"

"He's always home," I said. "He's a writer."

"Oh, yeah. Well, tell him I need to talk to him

about that storage room. It's important. And Finnegan?"

"Yes?"

"Don't mention anything I've said to Pryce, all right?"

"Sure. I mean, sure I won't."

"Good boy." Pablo sat down heavily on his couch. He set the two cans on the glass table. "And thanks for the mail." He reached for the package and started ripping open one of the edges.

"Well, good night," I said. "I mean, um, good morning."

"Yeah, good morning," said Pablo. He shook his head. "Chewed off by rats. Hey, don't forget to tell your uncle I need to talk to him."

"I won't."

"I think I need a knife for this," he said. He followed me toward the back door and walked into his kitchen with his package. I was just turning the doorknob when I heard him.

"What the—?"

Pablo was standing by the sink and staring at his dish drainer. Spoons and forks and knives were sticking out of a small white plastic bin. One of the spoons was different from the others. First, it was thicker than any normal spoon. Second, feathers were carved into the handle. Third, the spoon gleamed the same dull yellow as the Horizontal Man.

"What is this?" asked Pablo, pulling the spoon from the plastic bin.

Gold. Feathers. It was part of the treasure from Agualar. I knew it. I don't know how I knew it, but I knew it.

I snatched the spoon from Pablo's surprised fingers and ran into the back hall. The solid gold was as heavy as a baseball bat. I rushed into my kitchen, locked the door behind me, and jumped into my bed.

The spoon was mine. No one was going to steal it from me.

3
A Thief and a Witch

Later that morning, someone was knocking on our front door. I knew who it was. I clutched the golden spoon in my hand and stayed under the bed covers. I could hear Uncle Stoppard stumbling out of his bed and walking into the front of the apartment. Men's voices. Then footsteps walking back through the apartment. Footsteps getting louder and closer. There was a knock on my bedroom door.

"Finnegan," said Uncle Stoppard. "Are you awake?"

"No," I said. "And it belongs to me."

Uncle Stoppard came into the room. I could see Pablo's head poking through the door.

"Where is it, Finn?" asked Uncle Stoppard.

"Where's what?"

"The thing you said belongs to you. The spoon."

"We keep spoons in the kitchen," I said.

Uncle Stoppard's face looked very stern. "May I please see it, Finn?"

I hated having to give it to Uncle Stoppard. Especially with Pablo the Thief watching me.

"Where did you get this?" asked Uncle Stoppard.

"Ask him," I said, pointing to Pablo.

"He already told me about finding it in his kitchen."

"It's mine," I said.

"Finnegan—"

"Look at it," I said. "Doesn't it look like it belongs to the Horizontal Man?"

Pablo said, "That spoon belongs to the dead body in the basement?"

"No," I said. "The *other* Horizontal Man."

Pablo looked confused. Uncle Stoppard said to him, "I'll explain later. Actually, the markings on this spoon do look pre-Columbian."

"What's that?" asked Pablo.

"Before Columbus reached the New World. This spoon could have been made by American natives hundreds of years ago."

"You mean it's Mayan?" Pablo asked.

"No, it's *mine,*" I said.

Pablo and Uncle Stoppard looked at each other. "The Maya," explained Uncle Stoppard, "were the people who lived in Mexico hundreds of years ago. They probably made this artifact."

"And they lost it," I said. "And my parents found it. Finders keepers."

"How did this get in your kitchen, Pablo?" asked Uncle Stoppard.

Pablo shrugged his shoulders. "I have no idea. I'll ask my friend Larry about it."

"It's not his, either," I said.

Uncle Stoppard asked, "Mind if I keep this for a while?"

"Like forever?" I added.

"It's all right," said Pablo. "I'm going to stop by my friend's tonight after work. I'll ask if it belongs to him."

"It'll be safe over here." Uncle Stoppard stood up from my bed. "Finnegan, don't you have something to say?"

"Good-bye, Pablo," I said.

"I meant an apology."

"But it belongs to me."

"Finnegan—"

I stared down at my covers. "I'm sorry I ran out of your apartment last night," I said. "And I'm sorry about the spoon. Even though it's mine."

"I'll talk to you later, Pablo," said Uncle Stoppard.

Breakfast was very quiet. It was the first breakfast without raisins. Uncle Stoppard made plain waffles. The golden spoon lay gleaming on the kitchen table between us.

"I've never known you to act this way before, Finn." He stared at me over the thick rims of his glasses.

"The spoon is from Agualar."

"We don't know that for sure," he said. "Though I'll admit it does look like Maya work."

"Maybe we should ask a museum to examine it," I said. "Maybe they could tell for sure."

Uncle Stoppard groaned. "Yeah, a museum. How could I have been so stupid? I should have gotten rid of that stuff down there long ago. I promised Anna."

"You can't get at it now. The police have tape across the door."

A knock at the front door. It was Pablo again.

"I forgot to tell you," said Pablo. He handed Uncle Stoppard a shiny new key. "This is yours. I put a new lock on the storage room a couple days ago."

"That's your padlock?" said Uncle Stoppard.

Pablo nodded. "Last week, I was talking with the girls upstairs and they thought someone was trying to break into the basement. They noticed a few things missing. They got new locks for their bikes. So I thought I'd put a stronger lock on the storage room. I had a key for you, but I was so busy getting ready for the convention that I forgot to give it to you."

When Pablo left, Uncle Stoppard hung the shiny, new key on the hook by the back door. "Well, that's one mystery cleared up," he said.

"Maybe," I said. "And maybe Pablo was taking things out of that room, piece by piece. He only told you about the key because the police are involved. Just think, if I hadn't gone down there, all the treasure would be gone and we'd never know about it until it was too late."

"Eat your breakfast," said Uncle Stoppard.

I ate two more waffles. With each mouthful, I looked at the golden spoon and thought about the Maya and Mexico and Agualar.

"Is Pablo Mexican?" I asked.

"He's Hispanic," said Uncle Stoppard, clearing away the breakfast dishes. "I don't know if he's Mexican or not."

"What's the difference?"

"Hispanic means your ancestors come from anywhere in Latin America. Pablo's ancestors could be from Mexico or Costa Rica or Panama or—"

"I wonder if Pablo has ever been to Agualar," I said.

"You still think he stole the Horizontal Man?" asked Uncle Stoppard.

"It's gone," I said.

"Gone?"

I told Uncle Stop about my conversation with Pablo in his apartment late last night, and how the statue was missing from the glass coffee table.

"You shouldn't go in a stranger's apartment at night," said Uncle Stoppard.

"Pablo isn't a stranger," I said. "He might be a thief and a murderer, but he's not a stranger."

"You need evidence before you accuse someone, Finn. Evidence."

I pointed at the golden spoon. "There's evidence," I said.

Uncle Stoppard picked it up off the table. "I do like the idea you mentioned earlier."

"What idea?"

"That we keep our spoons in the kitchen." He placed the Agualar spoon in the kitchen drawer with the regular spoons and knives and forks. "It will be just as safe here as anywhere else in the apartment." He shut the drawer with a bang.

"But I don't like what Pablo said," said Uncle Stoppard.

"I don't like what Pablo *did*."

"You heard what he said about someone breaking into the basement. We've never had a problem with burglars before. Have you noticed anything missing, Finn?"

"Besides the Agualar treasure? No."

"Gosh, everything's happening all at once. First you see a statue that looks like the one in your photograph. And then—"

And then we heard another knock on our front door.

"Pablo again?" said Uncle Stoppard.

"Maybe he's going to confess to the murder," I said. "I'll hold the spoon."

"Leave the spoon right where I put it," said Uncle Stoppard.

It wasn't Pablo. It was Ms. Pryce. This morning she was wearing a black skirt, a black blouse, black tights, and black sandals. Her belt buckle was a silver skull. Ms. Pryce disproves the idea that vampires come out only at night.

"The cops came by," she said. She stood outside our front door, with her hands on her hips. "They wanted to let us know that they're finished with the crime scene. You're allowed to go back into the storage room."

"What should we do about the smell?" asked Uncle Stoppard.

Ms. Pryce sighed heavily. "I suppose you'll want me to clean it." She started walking down the stairs to her apartment. "I'm not sure what I can do about those bloodstains."

"Oh, by the way, Ms. Pryce. I heard we had a problem with someone breaking into the basement."

Ms. Pryce turned around on the steps below our landing. "Did the nurses tell you that?"

"I just heard about it," said Uncle Stoppard.

"I think," said Ms. Pryce, "that Miss Bellini and Miss Brazil misplaced some items and they think someone stole them."

"No burglars?" I asked.

"No broken windows or smashed locks or mysterious footprints in the flower beds," said Ms. Pryce. "No one broke into anything."

Someone broke into our storage room, I thought. I
watched Ms. Pryce's back disappear down the stairs,
and then I whispered to Uncle Stoppard. "Maybe she
could cast a spell and make the bloodstains invisible."

"Finnegan!"

"Well, she dresses like a witch."

"You shouldn't judge a book by its cover." Uncle
Stoppard closed and locked the front door. "Of
course, a witch might be useful right about now."

"Useful?" I said.

"Maybe she could help us get rid of the famous
Zwake Curse."

When my parents disappeared in Iceland years ago,
they were not the first victims of the Zwake family
curse. The first victim was my Aunt Verona. She was
with my parents down in Agualar. After the gold artifacts had been dug up, some of them began to disappear. Aunt Verona and my parents thought the thief
was one of the workers they had hired from the
nearby towns. Some of the Agualarans believed the
gold was cursed by the ancient Maya and that anyone
who tried to remove the gold would be doomed.

One day Aunt Verona was out canoeing on a
nearby river. Her empty, overturned canoe was found
hours later floating in the river. Aunt Verona's body
was never found.

More gold disappeared. Then a fierce tropical
storm, Hurricane Midge, forced my parents to flee
their campsite. Not long after that they returned to
Minneapolis, left me with Uncle Stoppard, and flew
off to Iceland. They were searching for the lost Viking
city of Tquuli. Weeks went by without anyone hearing

from them. A Norwegian rescue team found their footprints in the snow, footprints that stopped in the middle of nowhere. That was seven years ago.

The television and newspaper reporters called it the "Zwake Curse." They even predicted that something might happen to me, their son, the last member of the Zwake family. The curse wouldn't affect Uncle Stoppard because he's not a Zwake. He's my mom's brother. In fact, Uncle Stoppard isn't even a Sterling. That's just his fancy author name. His real last name is Bumpelmeyer. You can see why he changed it.

Uncle Stoppard told me all this after breakfast. He didn't want to tell me before because he thought I was too young. He knows I like to read about ghosts and haunted houses and zombies and stuff. But he thought learning about the curse might frighten me. Frighten me? Please. I'm thirteen years old.

"Curses are just superstitions," I said. "Right?"

"Right."

"Just pretend, just make-believe," I said.

"That's why I never talked much about your parents, or the treasure of Agualar, or your Aunt Verona. I didn't want you to learn about the curse and worry. But, I figure you're old enough to know about it now."

"Yeah. Old enough."

"Well, I'm off to the library this morning," said Uncle Stoppard.

"Are you nuts? You're going to leave me alone with a curse in the basement?"

"Finn, you just said—"

"Why are we going to the library?" I asked.

"*We* are going because *I* need to get some information on pygmies."

"Pygmies?"

"I was thinking of making the murderer in my next book a pygmy. Actually, they're called the Efe. Someone small enough to get into places a normal-sized person couldn't."

"But doesn't Mona already have a pygmy detective?"

Uncle Stoppard's face turned as red as a Nebraska football team. "So what? Mona doesn't have a monopoly on pygmies. Anyone can write about pygmies." Uncle Stoppard stomped into his bedroom and slammed the door.

Mona Trafalgar-Squeer is probably the most stunning mystery writer in the world. Next to Uncle Stoppard, of course. Critics call her the Queen of Crime, the Princess of Puzzles, the Baroness of Bafflement. Her detective is the superclever Revelation-of-St.-John Bugloop, the half-French, half-pygmy ex-priest with a trained meerkat for an assistant. His archnemesis is the one-eyed, seven-foot Duchess of De-Monica, who scours the world for a gem the exact color of her good eye. Mona's plots are the best. They are galactic. You can never figure out her puzzles until the last page. Mona was born in England and is still a British citizen, but she spends her summers in Minneapolis where she tools around on a giant silver Kawasaki, or spends months locked in her apartment overlooking the Mississippi River. So far, she's published five mysteries. Just like Uncle Stoppard. I don't know why, but for some reason she and Uncle Stop aren't exactly chums.

Uncle Stoppard came bouncing out of his room and into the hall. He was trying to yank on a pair of stiff, new jeans while he was ranting about Mona. "Queen of Crime?" Uncle Stoppard said. "Ha! It's a crime her books sell. Ow!" He tripped on a pant leg and fell in the hallway, knocking over a small bookcase and an umbrella stand. There aren't any umbrellas in the umbrella stand, but Uncle Stoppard thinks it's cool to own because Sherlock Holmes has one.

"I think I'm bleeding. Am I bleeding, Finn?"

"You're not bleeding."

"You hardly even looked at my head."

"Your hair is so short, I could see right away if you were bleeding."

Uncle Stoppard gently patted his head. "I probably have a concussion." He disappeared back into his bedroom.

My favorite book of Mona's is called *Castaways*, in which the villain is an evil doctor. The doctor secretly plans accidents so that his victims break an arm or a leg. Then, when the victims come to the doctor for help, he puts poison into the plaster cast. The poison slowly seeps into their bodies and kills them. Nobody can figure out how the poison gets into the victims.

"Mona's murders are too complicated," Uncle Stoppard said, coming out of the bedroom while wiggling into a white T-shirt. "Ouch!" He walked into the hall closet door. Maybe the Zwake Curse had landed on Uncle Stoppard.

"Are we taking the bus?" I asked.

"I was planning on riding my bike." He rubbed his head again. "That was before I realized you were afraid of the so-called Zwake Curse."

"Who's afraid?" I said. Just because three members

of my family had vanished under mysterious circumstances didn't mean that I was afraid.

"Riding the bus would be smarter than biking," said Uncle Stoppard. "I don't want to pass out on the street from a concussion."

"You're fine," I said.

He pulled on a shoulder bag and headed toward the back door. "Why aren't you getting ready?" he asked.

"I think I'll stay here."

"Come with me, Finn."

"I don't like the library."

"You *love* the library."

"I got stuff to do." I couldn't tell Uncle Stoppard why I had changed my mind.

"Stuff?" Uncle Stoppard grabbed his house keys off the kitchen table. "You're not planning on bothering Pablo some more, are you?"

"Pablo's at work."

"And stay out of the basement," he said.

"Basement? Why would I want to go down there?" I asked.

"Right," said Uncle Stoppard. "I'll see you in a few hours."

When Uncle Stoppard left, the apartment became spooky quiet. I kept thinking about the Zwake Curse. Maybe I should have gone with him, made sure he didn't have an accident on his bike. Make sure he didn't disappear like Mom and Dad and Aunt Verona.

Back in my bedroom, I stared at the photograph taken in Agualar seven years ago. Too bad I didn't have a photograph of Aunt Verona. I wondered what she looked like. Maybe there were some pictures in the stuff that Mom and Dad left with Uncle Stoppard.

Maybe there were more pictures of me. I'd find out soon enough.

I hadn't exactly promised Uncle Stoppard that I wouldn't go snooping in the basement. Not really. My exact words were a question, "Why would I go down there?" Answer: to find more stuff before it's stolen by our friendly neighbor.

The basement looked normal. It was dim and cool as always. Barely enough light came through the small windows high up on the walls. I pulled on the light chains along the way, just like last time. This time I held Pablo's new key in my hand. Then I realized I didn't need it; the door was still open. I ripped off the yellow police tape and stepped inside.

Last time, I didn't even notice what was inside the room. I had only been looking at the body. There were still shiny black bloodstains on the floor. I tried to step around these, while looking for our stuff. I figured one side belonged to Pablo and one side to Uncle Stoppard and me. But which was which?

Then I saw a cardboard box with "Agualar Expedition" written with a marker on the side. I pulled it onto the floor and opened it up. It was full of paper and notebooks and those fat little photo envelopes you get from the camera store. I opened one envelope and dozens of colorful photos spilled out. There were pictures of dark-skinned men and women digging in the ground and eating at tables set under tents. One picture showed a couple of strange men holding the Horizontal Man and pointing at it. They looked very excited. They must have just dug it up.

There were pictures of lots of strangers, but no pictures of my parents. Another wrinkled photo showed

me. It must have been hot, I was wearing only shorts.
I wondered what I would have looked like in a little
furry snowsuit. Icelandic kids probably look like Minnesota kids.

Then I found it. A fat, purple book that turned out
to be my dad's diary. I turned to the back of the book.
The last pages in Mona's mysteries always explain the
puzzle. Maybe my dad's last pages would explain
things. I read:

May 13

*Anna and I went down to the Pellagro River
again today. We went back to the spot where Verona's canoe was found. Anna brought a small bouquet of flowers she had bought in the village. We
placed it on the riverbank.*

*The workers blame Verona's disappearance on
the old Maya curse. Anna and I don't believe in
superstitions. And I think it's interesting how people are selective with their superstitions. Verona,
they say, disappeared because of the Maya. But
no one blamed the curse when Antonio Morado
vanished. The workers say he left because he didn't
like working for Americans. Funny, Morado certainly liked American money. Anna and I are the
only ones who know the real explanation for his
disappearance. I feel sorry for Verona for so
many reasons.*

*Sometimes accidents happen. We can't always
explain why they happen, but we can learn from
them. Anna and I have decided to learn from this
tragedy. We are going to leave Finnegan with*

*Anna's brother in Minneapolis. Our jobs are too
dangerous and unpredictable for us to be chasing
around the globe with a small child. If anything
happened to Finnegan, as it happened to Verona,
I would never forgive myself.*

There was a small crackling sound somewhere in
the basement. Rats, I thought. Then I heard it again.
Didn't those rodents get enough to eat last time? I
was feeling jumpy because of the curse. Why did
Uncle Stoppard have to tell me about it anyway? He
knows I hate stuff like that.

Who was that Antonio fellow that Dad wrote
about? And why did he leave the expedition? And
what were those "many reasons" that made Dad feel
sorry for Verona? He felt bad not only because she
died, but because of something else.

There was another crackling sound. No, it wasn't
crackling. It was short and raspy. Like a bike chain
switching gears. Chain! That's what it was. The light
chains. Someone was tugging them off one by one.
And whoever it was was getting closer to the storage room.

"Hello," I called out. There was no reply.

"Uncle Stoppard?" I heard another chain being
pulled. The light outside the storage room door was
growing dimmer.

I stood up from where I had been sitting on the
floor. Why didn't I stay up in the apartment like Uncle
Stoppard asked me? Why did he have to go to that
stupid library and read about some stupid pygmies?

Footsteps echoed in the basement. Someone was
trying to be quiet, but I could hear them walking

closer to the storage room. I tiptoed closer to the
door. Very gently I placed a hand on the door. I was
going to push it open farther.

The door pushed back.

It swung shut and trapped me inside the room. I
heard a scraping sound. The padlock was being
snapped shut.

I leaned against the door, but it was shut tight.

I was locked inside. Just like the man on the floor
with the rat turds and the blue legs. The horizontal
man.

4
Missing V

Do rats have three meals a day? Would the tiny beasts that got the horizontal man—not the statue, but the dead guy stretched out flat on the storage room floor—come back for seconds? Or for dessert? After the storage room door shut, I heard the footsteps go away. I yelled for help. Uncle Stoppard should be able to hear me through the floor. Then I remembered he was at the library.

Maybe someone would come downstairs to do laundry. After all, Mr. Barrymore needed to clean his kilt.

Nobody came. My luck, everyone had clean clothes that day.

Uncle Stoppard would be home in a few hours. I could try yelling again later. As long as I was in the storage room, I thought I might as well look through our stuff.

Boxes from Agualar were piled in a corner. Some boxes just contained old clothes. Women's shoes and men's pants and summer shirts. There was even more gold. Nothing as big as the Horizontal Man, but there were two gold knives with those same feathers carved on the handles, and a golden dish as big as a cereal bowl. Maybe this evidence would convince the police that the spoon I found in Pablo's kitchen belongs to me. Well, belongs to the Zwake family. I wrapped the knives and the dish in some of the old summer clothes. Then I stuffed them all deep into a box marked "Taxes." That should keep them safe for a while. At least until Uncle Stoppard and I can think of a better hiding place. Or until Uncle Stoppard finds that address for the Ackerberg Institute.

It was hard to tell how much time passed in the room. After a while I read some more of my dad's diary. Some of it was written in another language. I guess he was practicing his Spanish.

Then, I found the day when Aunt Verona disappeared.

April 2

As Charles Dickens might have said, today was the best of days and the worst of days. First, the worst part. Verona disappeared. Jose and Fernando found her empty canoe on the wide Pellagro River by the bat cliffs. Anna and I are hoping that she may still be alive. She may be on the other side of the river, trying to find a way to get across. Maybe she hit her head and has amnesia. Or maybe she hiked to the town of Chuca, where the only bridge for miles around is located, and somehow the canoe got loose on the river. It is too dark now to keep looking for her. In the morning, we will send out another search party. Anna is very upset. We are praying that Verona is sleeping safely in Chuca, waiting for morning to catch a ride back into camp.

Today, we found the Horizontal Man in location number 12. It is beautiful, and matches the descriptions of him we read in the old scrolls. The decorations match the other artifacts we have found. He is smaller, but much heavier than Finnegan, fourteen inches long, seven inches wide, and nine inches high. When we showed it to Finn, the first thing he did was bite it. He must have seen me do the same sort of thing with gold coins we find, testing them. Luckily for him, gold is a soft metal. A 1,000-year-old Maya statue now has teeth marks from a modern American kid.

Teeth marks! That would prove the Horizontal Man belongs to me. The police could match my teeth to the bite marks. Now all I have to do is find the statue.

April 3

The search parties have had no luck. Verona is still missing. Tomorrow Anna and I are driving into town to see if the State Department can help us.

Unfortunately, we have also lost the plate we discovered two days ago. With so many people working on this dig, there is the slight possibility that someone cleaning or cataloging the plate has misplaced it. Anna thinks it will turn up. I believe there is a thief among us. The same thief who stole the golden crocodile last week.

*　　*　　*

So Mom and Dad had problems with a thief, too. Maybe I should check out Pablo's apartment for a golden croc.

And stole my lucky Blackfoot hunting knife, too.

Blackfoot was the name of an Indian tribe. I didn't know Dad had a lucky hunting knife. I didn't know Dad hunted. Except for dead stuff, that is.

April 4

Disappointment!!

Dad had underlined the word three times.

I turned the page and a photo fell into my lap. It showed a woman with short, dark hair and freckles, smiling and squinting at the camera. I turned the photo over and read, in my dad's handwriting: Verona, Agualar.

Met with a Mr. Perez from the State Department. He says they are unable to help us. Unwilling, is more like it. Since Verona's disappearance appears to be an accident, the authorities have no reason to investigate. I asked if he could request the local police to help in our search. Perez said he would make a few calls.

Returned to camp around 1:00. All work at the site has stopped. Anna and I organized three more search parties this afternoon. One group covered the riverbank. Anna drove up to Chuca in the Jeep. I canoed with Tomas and Pablo across the river.

Pablo? As in Pablo DeSoto? In Agualar? Maybe he followed me to Minneapolis, and was waiting for the right time to steal the rest of the treasure. And maybe Aunt Verona wasn't missing at all. Maybe Pablo killed her and left her canoe drifting in the river so Dad and Mom would think she had an accident.

Across the Pellagro and upstream of the bat cliffs where we first spotted Verona's canoe, I found signs of a recent campfire and empty food tins. No signs of V. Tomas discovered marks along the shore that could have been made by a canoe being dragged on the sand. I haven't seen any of the locals using canoes. The marks on the shore could have been made by Verona's canoe. But the marks may indicate that Verona simply landed here before her accident. The campfire and tins could have been left by anyone.

During the last several months, V. and I have not been getting along very well. I should never have asked her to join the Agualar dig. She hated the last dig up in Alberta, always complaining about the cold and the Canadian customs. But she didn't complain about the money. She said how the Ackerberg Institute paid much better than the Army ever did. And I knew she could use the cash. Plus, she was very good at cataloging and referencing. She had a great eye for detail. (I just realized I've been using the past tense when describing Verona. Anna would say that I need to "verbalize more positively.")

Anna knows that my sister and I have always rubbed each other the wrong way. This is a terrible

*thing to think, but if V. doesn't turn up, I will
certainly not miss her complaining and her
selfishness.*

I hope she turns up.

*Anna appears to be in shock. She hasn't eaten
dinner or supper today. When I ask her to talk,
she turns away. Tonight, while she slept, I spent
two hours down on the shore by myself—in vain—
searching for clues.*

Searching for clues? I looked up from where I was
sitting on the floor. Half of the storage room belonged
to Pablo. Maybe there was a clue in this room, some
piece of evidence stashed among Pablo's belongings
that would tell me more about the so-called Mr.
DeSoto.

Pablo didn't store much in the storage room. A couple skis and ski poles leaned against the wall. Ice
skates hung from a rusty hook, next to a dusty tennis
racket. I went through a few boxes but only found
some boring-looking papers with numbers all over
them and some old checks. Nothing important.

I heard someone walking upstairs. Uncle Stoppard
must be home. I yelled again, but the walking just
continued. Maybe he can't hear me. I looked at Pablo's ski poles and got an idea. I grabbed one by the
handle and pounded it against the ceiling of the storage room. Someone should hear this. I kept pounding.
Then the handle slipped from my hands. The ski pole
was stuck, the pointy end jammed into a crack in the
ceiling. Great!

The footsteps had stopped. Maybe Uncle Stoppard
was coming downstairs after all. I felt in my pocket

to make sure I still had the key. I would need to slip it under the door for Uncle Stoppard to unlock the padlock.

I picked up my dad's diary, I wanted to read more of it upstairs. Then I heard someone outside the door. "Hey!" I yelled. The door flew open.

"What is all this racket?"

It was Ms. Pryce. She glared at me and then looked at the ski pole dangling from the ceiling in the middle of the room. "What is that doing there?"

"Thanks for rescuing me, Ms. Pryce," I said.

"That's a ski pole," she said. "Do you have any idea how expensive those things are? Those are not toys."

"I was trying to get help," I said, clutching my dad's diary. "I've been locked in here for hours."

"What kind of game are you playing?"

"It's not a game. The door was locked."

Ms. Pryce shook her blue head. "If the door was locked, then how did I open it?"

I squeezed past her and looked at the padlock. It dangled loosely on the metal loop in the door. She was right, the lock was open. "But I heard it snap shut."

"I don't know how you could hear anything through that racket you were making," said Ms. Pryce.

"I was calling for help."

"You woke me up the other night with all your thumping, too."

"What do you mean?" I asked.

"When you were playing in here a couple nights ago. I woke up in the middle of the night and heard a big thump."

"I wasn't playing in here at night. And I'm not playing now. I was trying to get someone's attention."

"Well, you got my attention." Ms. Pryce hadn't moved from where she stood in the open doorway. She glanced down at the black stains on the storage room floor. "It's disrespectful to be fooling around in here," she said. "Why anyone would come back inside here after—" Ms. Pryce turned away. She looked like she might throw up again.

I shut the storage door behind me and headed toward the stairs. "Thanks again," I said.

Ms. Pryce was leaning against the wall. She jerked a thumb over her shoulder and said, "Don't leave your pole stuck back in there."

"I'll fix it later."

"Your uncle has to pay for any damage to the ceiling."

"Don't worry," I said, climbing the stairs. "He'll pay."

Uncle Stoppard paid all right.

Uncle Stoppard still was not home. Whose footsteps did I hear? Was it just the apartment creaking or old water pipes gurgling? For two microseconds, I thought a burglar was in our apartment. I saw the bookshelf in our hallway tipped over, books scattered on the floor, the Sherlock Holmes umbrella stand lying on its side. Then I remembered Uncle Stoppard's noisy, crashing departure for the library.

Footsteps squeaked across the ceiling above me. That was the apartment where the two nurses lived, Miss Brazil and Miss Bellini. Could they have heard or seen anything unusual in the past couple of hours?

I threw Dad's diary on my bed, walked up the back stairs and knocked on their door. A moment later it was opened by a gigantic piece of Easter candy. Miss Brazil—or was it Miss Bellini?—was wrapped in pink sweat pants, a pink sweatshirt, and pink socks. A pink headband held back her fluffy, golden hair. White and gold letters on her sweatshirt spelled "Get in the Pink." If Ms. Pryce looked like a vampire or witch, this lady looked like a fairy princess.

"Yes?"

"Hi, uh, I'm Finnegan Zwake from—"

"You're the boy from downstairs?"

"Yeah. Um, I was wondering if you were downstairs in the basement."

"The basement?"

"Just a little while ago."

The fairy princess got a funny look on her face. "You heard him," she said.

"Heard who?"

"The burglar. The person who's been taking stuff from the basement."

"Ms. Pryce says there isn't a burglar."

The princess folded her pink arms across the white and gold letters. "Then who broke into your storage room? Giant mice? Oh, sorry."

A picture of a giant raisin flashed through my brain. "That's okay," I said.

"Do you think he's still down there?" Her voice sounded shaky.

"Ms. Pryce is the only one down there right now. But, I, um, thought I heard someone else a few hours ago."

"Gosh. I wonder if Alison heard or saw anything— she's my roommate; my name's Joan, by the way— Alison went down there a few hours ago to take a wheel off her bike. She had to take it to the repair shop."

Maybe Alison saw the person who locked me in the storage room. I don't care what Ms. Pryce said, that door was locked. I heard the lock snap shut, and all my shoving and pushing couldn't open the door.

"There's something strange happening in this building," said Joan. "It used to feel so safe. Sorry, I don't mean to scare you. Do you think we should call the police—er, what was your name again?"

"Why are you calling the police, now?" A new voice streamed up the stairway. Footsteps trudged slowly upward. Joan looked at me and said, "It's her. My roommate."

Alison was tall and muscular like a guy. She had short dark hair and was wearing bike shorts and a neon green tank top. She looked like she could outrun Uncle Stoppard.

"Where's your wheel?" asked Joan.

"I already put it on the bike," said Alison. "I got back a few minutes ago."

"How much did it cost to get fixed?"

"Don't even ask," said Alison. "I have poured so much money into that bike."

"Why don't you buy another one?" I asked.

Alison looked at me carefully. "Who are you?"

"Finnegan."

"He's the boy who lives downstairs," said Joan.

"You want to know why I don't buy a new bike?" asked Alison. "What does your mother do for a living?"

"She's an archeologist."

"Really? Ask her if she makes as much money as a *male* archeologist."

Joan put a hand on my shoulder. "Finnegan thinks he heard the burglar downstairs a little while ago. About the time you were taking the wheel off."

"The burglar, huh?" asked Alison.

"Or the murderer," I said.

"Maybe the burglar and the murderer are the same person," Joan said.

"Did you get a good look at him?" Alison asked me.

"It could be a *her*," suggested her roommate.

"Not likely," Alison said, sneering. "Ninety-six percent of all killers are male."

How did she know that?

"I didn't see anyone," I said. "I heard someone moving around, turning off the lights."

Joan shivered in her pink sweatsuit. "Creepy."

"The lights were fine when I was down there," said Alison.

Alison must have been working on her bike while I was reading Dad's diary. Reading and slipping a wheel off a bike are both quiet activities. It's weird that we each didn't realize the other person was down there; I could have escaped from the storage room earlier. I could have yelled and slipped the key underneath the door to Alison. Then she could have unlocked the padlock. Wait. How was the padlock unlocked before Ms. Pryce opened the door? I had the key in my pocket the whole time. Is there a second key floating around somewhere?

"Maybe we should go check our stuff," said Joan. "See if anything is missing."

"Were you in the basement by yourself?" asked Alison.

I nodded.

"Where's your dad?"

"He's in Iceland with my mom."

"Iceland!"

"They're looking for a lost city."

Alison glanced at her roommate, then said, "They just left you by yourself?"

"I'm staying with my Uncle Stoppard."

"Oh, I see," said Alison. "Stoppard, hmm. That's an unusual name."

"It's not his real name," I said. "It's his pen name."

Joan gasped. "Pen name? His last name isn't Sterling, is it?"

"Yeah, Sterling," I said.

Miss Brazil and Miss Bellini rushed into their apartment. I felt completely forgotten. I stood there, not moving, like one of those little statues on someone's front lawn.

I stared at their back door. I stared at the lock. Then I remembered—of course there was a second key to the padlock for the storage room. Pablo had the other key. But why would Pablo quietly tiptoe downstairs and unlock the storage room without opening the door? If he wanted something from inside, why did he leave? If he came down to rescue me, why not let me know the door was unlocked? Unless it was Pablo who locked me inside the room in the first place. But, why let me back out? Was there a reason for keeping me in that room for a short period of time?

The two nurses rushed back. Each of them held a thick paperback book.

"*This* Stoppard Sterling?" asked Alison.

One book cover showed a pair of bloodstained blue shoes trapped in a block of ice. The other had an ice-covered casket with a skeleton holding a bouquet of dead flowers. I recognized Uncle Stoppard's two best mysteries: *Cold Feet* and *Sneezing and Coffin.*

"That's him," I said.

Joan stared at her roommate. "I don't believe it. He's right below our very feet."

"Our *cold* feet," said Alison. Both of them laughed. They were so excited about fake murders that they had forgotten all about the real murderer.

"Your uncle is famous," said Joan.

"We love his books," said Alison.

"Have you seen Pablo around?" I asked.

Alison ignored me and flipped to the back of the book she was holding and read the inside cover. " 'Stoppard Sterling is the author of four previous mysteries, including *Cold on the Carpet, Cold Shoulders, Cold Cuts,* and *Sneezing and Coffin.*' " Joan grinned and waved her copy of *Sneezing and Coffin.* Alison continued reading: " 'Mr. Sterling is a two-time winner of the Minnesota Book Award for Best Mystery. He lives in Minneapolis, where he is a part-time runner and full-time uncle to his nephew, Finnegan.' "

The words that Alison read out loud I already knew by heart. I remember the day Uncle Stoppard wrote them about himself, because that was the same day he asked me to take a picture of him with his new Olympus camera. The photo of Uncle Stop, the one printed at the back of all those thousands of copies, is the one I snapped of him sitting in our sunroom. Since it was his first book photo and he wanted to look good, Uncle Stop was nervous that day; he changed shirts twelve times. It's a close-up, so you can only see part of his shirt anyway. My name is printed sideways next to his picture. It's called a photo credit.

Alison looked at me again. "Finnegan. That's you?"

"Yeah."

"So, what's he like?" asked Joan.

"He likes to run," said Alison.

"How do you know that?" asked Joan.

"I just read it." Alison waved the bio of Uncle Stoppard in her friend's face. "Didn't you just hear me read that he's a part-time runner?"

"Oh, yeah."

"I have an idea." Alison was smiling. "Let's send him a pair of blue shoes, like in his book. We could send him some blue sneakers. I'll bet no one's thought of that."

"That would be fun," said Joan. "I'll bet he'd get a real kick out of that."

"A kick," I said.

"I'll bet he's going to write about that dead body in the basement," said Alison.

Joan frowned, shaking her head. "Not in front of the kid."

"That's all right," I said. "I was the one who found the body."

"You?" said Joan.

"And I didn't throw up, either."

"Poor Mr. Barrymore," said Joan.

"He sure made a mess," said Alison.

All three of us looked over at Mr. Barrymore's

door, about ten feet away on the other side of the landing. "Uncle Stoppard said that Mr. Barrymore probably felt so embarrassed he could have *kilt* himself."

The two nurses looked at each other and burst out laughing. Which is Miss Brazil and which is Miss Bellini?

"Your uncle sounds like fun," said Joan.

"Tell him he's our favorite mystery writer," said Alison. "Next to Mona Trafalgar-Squeer."

"Don't tell him that," Joan said with a wink.

"I won't."

"You think he would autograph these books for us?" asked Joan.

"Sure, I'll ask him when he gets home. He should be back any minute."

A loud piercing scream shot up the stairway and bounced off the walls.

"I think," I said, "I hear him now."

5
Uncle Stoppard Gets the Point

I rushed down the stairs with the nurses right behind me. I ran through our apartment back door, banged down our hallway, jumped over the books still scattered on the floor, reached the living room, and froze. Uncle Stoppard was hopping up and down on one foot and yelling.

"I stepped on something in that stupid hallway," he shouted. "Am I bleeding? I'm bleeding, right."

"No, Uncle Stoppard," I said. "You're not—oh, wow! Yes, you are bleeding."

"I am?" He fell down onto the couch, holding his injured foot.

Joan appeared in our hallway, her face as pink as her sweatsuit. "May we come in?" she said. "Are you all right? We heard—oh, you're bleeding."

"Finn," said Uncle Stoppard. "Get me a bandage."

Joan kneeled down by the couch. "Let me look. I'm a nurse."

"I'm a nurse, too," said Alison, waving.

"From upstairs?" Uncle Stoppard asked.

Joan nodded. "Here, let's pull off that sock. My, you punctured it all right."

Uncle Stoppard's face paled. "Punctured?"

"Punctured?" I said.

"Just a small one," said Joan. "What did you step on?"

"Who knows?" said Uncle Stoppard. "That stupid shelf in the hallway fell over this morning. I suppose something spilled on the floor."

Alison stepped into the living room. "Anything I can do?"

"Yeah," said Joan. "Go upstairs and bring down our emergency kit."

Alison ran back down the hall and out the back door. I followed her partway and searched the floor for whatever had put a hole in Uncle Stoppard's foot. The bookcase had been knocked out of its usual place that morning. A rectangular outline of dust showed where the case normally sat jammed next to the wall. I started picking up books and putting them back into their shelves when I saw it: the object that Uncle Stoppard had stepped on. Sticking up through a small crack in the floorboards, half-hidden by a book, was the sharp point of a ski pole. There was blood on it.

"Finn, where are you?" called Uncle Stoppard.

"Um, just cleaning."

The point of the ski pole was stuck inside the dusty outline made by the bookshelf. When Uncle Stoppard had stumbled into the hallway earlier in the day, he had knocked the shelf out of its usual spot and revealed the crack in the floorboards. If he hadn't been so upset about Mona Trafalgar-Squeer this morning, or if he had put on his T-shirt before rushing out of his bedroom (and crashing into the wall), none of this would have happened.

Alison came back and pushed past me on her way

to the living room. I could hear her and Joan helping clean and wrap Uncle Stoppard's foot.

"Do you need any help, Finn?" called Uncle Stoppard.

"I'm fine," I said. I grabbed a heavy hardcover book and slammed it against the point of the ski pole.

"What's that noise?" asked Uncle Stoppard.

"Um, it's—" I looked at the book. "It's *Philosophy and Art in Ancient India.*"

"Sounds pretty heavy," said Joan, also from the living room.

Not heavy enough. Even after slamming it with everything India and I had in us, the ski pole point stayed put. It didn't budge a micro-millimeter. The book, however, now had a deep puncture in its back cover. Right through the Taj Mahal. Maybe Uncle Stop wouldn't notice.

"Someone's knocking at the back door, Finn," called Uncle Stoppard.

"That's just me. I'm still cleaning."

India was no help at all. The ceramic umbrella stand, however, looked good and solid. I grabbed it with both hands and slammed its bottom against the bloody pole point. It worked. The umbrella stand hit the floor, shoving the ski pole down into the storage room. Only a small hole remained in the floorboards. I pushed the bookcase back to its original position, covering up the hole and, I hoped, the evidence. I reshelved the rest of the books, picked up some loose change that was scattered on the floor, and gently placed the umbrella stand next to the wall.

I walked back into the living room. Uncle Stoppard's bandaged foot was stretched out straight in front of him, resting on the coffee table. Joan and Alison sat on the couch on either side of him.

"Did you find anything?" Uncle Stoppard asked.

"These are yours," I said, dropping some coins onto the living room coffee table.

"Have you had a tetanus shot?" asked Alison.

"I don't remember," said Uncle Stoppard.

"Well, you should probably have your doctor take a look at that foot," she said.

Joan stood up. "Mr. Sterling, could you do us a favor? We'd love to get your autograph."

"Oh, you've read my books?"

"I really loved *Cold Feet,*" said Alison.

Uncle Stoppard grinned. "Thanks. People seem to like that book the best. Oh, and look over there. You'll get a kick out of that." He pointed to the mountains of envelopes and packages in our front room.

"Fan mail?" asked Joan.

"Fans of *Cold Feet*. People think it's cute to send me blue shoes because of the murderer's blue shoes in the book. I don't know what puts weird ideas like that into people's heads."

Alison and Joan looked at each other.

"Sure is getting late," said Alison.

"Stay off your foot for a little while," said Joan. "Don't get up. We'll see ourselves out."

Uncle Stoppard lay back down on the couch. For the rest of the afternoon, he watched TV and I was his servant. I fetched him tons of snacks, oceans of diet pop, and mountains of pillows for his back.

"This is silly," he said, munching his way through a bag of chips. "I'm not an invalid."

"Miss Bellini said to stay off your foot," I said. "I mean, I think she said it. It could have been Miss Brazil." I should take a peek at their mailboxes and check out who's who.

"You must have other things to do, Finn."

"What things? It's vacation."

"I just can't imagine what I stepped on."

"A nail," I suggested.

"Where would a nail come from? You're sure you didn't find any—?"

"Nope. Nothing."

"Maybe I should take a look." He stood up. "I don't want you stepping on something and hurting yourself."

"I wonder if a person can bleed to death from a puncture wound," I said.

"Bleed to death?" said Uncle Stoppard.

"If a person stands up, does all the blood rush to his feet?"

Uncle Stoppard sat back down on the couch. "I think I'll have some more diet pop."

"Aren't you going to go look in the hallway?" I asked. "Gosh, I sure don't want to step on whatever hurt you."

"Wear shoes," he said.

The second, and worst, disaster of the day happened while we were watching TV later that night. Someone knocked at our door.

"Mr. Sterling?" It was Detective Linker. This time she looked more official. She was wearing a dark suit and a trench coat just like detectives in the movies. But she had earrings on again. Tiny gold nightsticks. There were two uniforms in the hall behind her. Neither of them was Jared the fingerprint cop with the yellow mustache. They were both new: a woman cop in glasses and a man cop with splotchy cheeks that were always red, like he was embarrassed or had been running hard. They both wore those incredibly shiny cop shoes.

Detective Linker waved a piece of paper in my face. Uncle Stoppard watched from his seat on the couch.

"I have a warrant to search your apartment," said the detective. "May we come in?"

We had to let them in. Detective Linker was only asking to be polite. For the next hour or so, the three officers searched our apartment. The detective explained that since the dead body was found in our storage room, we were considered potential suspects.

"But Pablo had a key, too," I said.

"We also have a warrant to search Mr. DeSoto's apartment," said Detective Linker, waving a second piece of paper from a coat pocket.

"Good. Maybe you'll find more stuff he stole."

"Finn!" said Uncle Stoppard.

"I don't know why *we* should be suspects. We don't even know who that dead guy is."

"Everyone in this building is considered a potential suspect," said the detective. "Everyone in the building had access to the basement."

"Pablo is the one who put that new lock on our storage door," I said.

"That's right," said Uncle Stoppard. Then he explained how Pablo forgot to give us the new key before he went on his business trip.

Detective Linker wrote down the new info in her

notepad. "I'd like to take a look at your key to that padlock," she said.

One of the police officers, I mean, uniforms, came into the living room. "We found something," he said to the detective. The officer gave Uncle Stoppard a funny look. If I had been Uncle Stoppard, I would have given it back.

I followed the detective and the uniform into the hallway. I didn't throw up when I saw that dead body in our storage room, but now I almost did. The other uniform, the woman in glasses, was holding the umbrella stand in her gloved hands. She held it out for the detective to inspect. Detective Linker bent her head down and stared at the base of the stand. Then she straightened back up.

"Blood?" she said.

The uniforms nodded.

Detective Linker grabbed the stand and returned to the living room. Uncle Stoppard was still sitting on the couch, even though he had turned off the TV when the police had arrived.

"Is this yours?" asked the detective.

"Uh, yes," said Uncle Stoppard. "It's an umbrella stand."

"Do you always have it in the hallway?"

"Ever since I bought it, about three years ago. Is there a problem?"

"There's blood on the bottom of it, Mr. Sterling."

"Blood!"

"Do you know whose it is?"

"It's his," I said.

"His?" asked the detective.

"Uncle Stoppard stepped on something in the hall-way and cut himself."

"I didn't step on the umbrella stand, Finn."

"Sure you did."

"I stepped on something sharp. The umbrella stand is smooth."

Detective Linker handed the stand to one of the uniforms who placed it in a brown grocery bag. "We'll need to take it for examination."

Uncle Stoppard nodded nervously. "Of course."

Then the second officer came into the living room. I thought I was going to be sick again. He was holding the golden Maya spoon from the kitchen.

"Is this yours, too?" asked the detective.

"Yes," said Uncle Stoppard.

"Actually, it belongs to me," I said. "My parents found it in Agualar. That's near Mexico. And since now they're in Iceland, all their stuff is mine."

Detective Linker looked at me. Then she looked at the spoon. Then she looked at me again. "And does the blood on this spoon belong to you, too?"

More blood? How did blood get on the golden spoon?

"It must belong to the dead guy," I said. "And then after Pablo killed him, he took the spoon back to his kitchen."

"Pablo again?" said Detective Linker.

"I found the spoon in Pablo's kitchen. It was in his dish rack."

"I don't think," said the detective, "that someone would use this spoon for eating a bowl of cereal."

"He was probably trying to wash off the blood," I

said. "That's why it was in the kitchen. It must be the murder weapon."

"The victim was hit with a large, heavy object," said the detective. "But we are going to need this for evidence, too."

"That belongs to me," I said.

Detective Linker turned to Uncle Stoppard. "May I see that key to your storage room?"

Uncle Stoppard got up and walked, with a slight limp, to the kitchen. He was about to lift the key off its hook, when the detective told him not to touch it. The guy uniform took it and dropped it into another plastic bag.

"Fingerprints," explained the detective.

Our back door opened and the lady uniform walked in. I didn't even notice that she had left our apartment. She jerked her head in the direction of Pablo's apartment. "No one answers the door," she said.

Detective Linker looked angry. "We'll come back later. Let's check the basement again."

I thought everyone else in the building was a potential suspect. Why weren't the officers going upstairs to question the nurses? Or Mr. Barrymore? What about our broomstick-riding caretaker? Maybe Detective Linker really did believe that Uncle Stoppard or Pablo killed that stranger in the basement.

I followed the three police officers into the basement. I stood by the washing machines as they walked over to our storage room door.

"When do I get my spoon back?" I asked.

"Let's check out the key," said Detective Linker. "And see if it fits."

"I don't think we have to, Lieutenant," said one of

the uniforms. The storage room door was slightly
open; I had forgotten to lock it after Ms. Pryce liber-
ated me that afternoon. The woman uniform pulled a
flashlight from her belt. She waved its beam into the
dark storage space. That's weird. When I left the storage room, the light was still on. Maybe Ms. Pryce had
switched it off in order to save electricity. I wormed
my way next to the detective to see what the flashlight revealed.

"What is that?" asked Detective Linker.

"I think," said the uniform, "it's a ski pole."

Great. The same stupid ski pole. The one that Uncle
Stoppard had stepped on. The one that got blood on
the bottom of the umbrella stand. It was now sticking
out of the back of a man's body on the floor of the
storage room. A new horizontal man, a man I knew:
Pablo the Thief.

Someone screamed upstairs.

At first I thought it was Uncle Stoppard stepping
on something else I left lying around on the floor.
Then, a microsecond later, I realized the scream belonged to a woman.

Since I was closest to the back steps, I raced up
ahead of the police officers. Ms. Pryce was standing
by the door to Pablo's apartment. She looked pale
and her shoulders were shaking.

"Burglar," she said. "Out the back door." Ms. Pryce
pointed a shivery finger to the back door of our building which led out to the alley.

"He ran out the door?" I asked.

"She," nodded Ms. Pryce. "She ran."

The night air in the alley was warm and humid. I

could hear the hum of an air conditioner from the building next door. At the far end of the alley, a figure raced away on a bicycle.

The uniform with the splotchy cheeks ran out next to me. His face was real red, and he puffed hard. "Careful, son," he said.

"She's down there," I pointed. "Someone on a bike."

"How do you know it's her?" he asked.

Good question. But I didn't want to waste any time. I ran back into the building and grabbed my bike from the back hallway. I always have it leaning against the wall next to our back door. By the time I walked it outside, the police were already seat-belted in their white squad car and turning on the blinking blue lights.

I pedaled as fast as I could. The alley slopes down from our apartment to the side street. I could smell lilac bushes and rotting garbage and cat litter as I rushed past other apartment buildings and houses. A few spooky shapes that looked like huge coffins turned into tarp-covered boats as I rode past them. At the end of the alley, I stopped and looked right and left. The other bike was nowhere in sight.

I don't know how long I was riding. I just kept pedaling up and down the streets, looking and listening for another bicycle. Nada. Not a bike in sight.

I saw the two lilac bushes at the end of our alley and decided to head on back. From this direction the alley was uphill, so I pedaled faster and shot toward the lilacs.

A car without its headlights on was barreling down the alley and heading straight toward me.

My legs were still pedaling forward, but my bike flew backward. A strong hand grabbed the back of my T-shirt. I heard the pig-squeal of brakes. The car door flew open and out popped a woman.

"Watch where you're going!" Ms. Pryce screamed at me.

"You should be more careful, kid," came an unfamiliar voice. I turned around and saw two guys and a dog on a purple leash. One of them, a blond guy, had yanked me and my bike out of the car's deadly path.

"Wow, sorry," I said.

"Just be more careful," said the guy again. His dog licked my knees.

"I could have been killed."

"You could have damaged my car," yelled Ms. Pryce.

"I was looking for the burglar."

"Burglar?" said the blond guy.

"That must be why all the cop cars are out," said his friend, a bald guy with a leather motorcycle jacket and a white T-shirt.

"Forget about the burglar," said Ms. Pryce. "The police are looking for you."

My heart froze. The cops knew about the umbrella stand. Maybe they think I killed Pablo with the ski pole. After all, my fingerprints would be on it. And Ms. Pryce would tell them she saw me fooling around with the pole earlier in the day. I even had a motive: Pablo was stealing my stuff. I wonder if there's a world record for the youngest person to be jailed for murder.

The blond guy pointed to Ms. Pryce's headlights. "Your lights aren't on."

"What do the police want me for?" I said.

"They're taking your uncle downtown. They think he wanted to get rid of DeSoto."

"DeSoto?" said the blond guy.

"Isn't that a type of old car?" asked the bald guy.

The blond guy nodded. "A collector's item. The kid's uncle must be a car thief." Their dog kept licking my knees.

"But Uncle Stoppard didn't do anything," I said.

"If you're lucky, they'll put you in a foster home," said Ms. Pryce. "It's a good thing DeSoto wasn't killed, or your uncle would have two murders on his hands."

"Pablo's not dead?"

Ms. Pryce squinted at the side of her car where my bike had bumped it. "You scraped the paint. Your uncle will have to pay for this, too." Then she squinted at me. "Hmm, the nut doesn't fall too far from the tree," she said.

"But the burglar," I said. "You saw the burglar. That proves Uncle Stoppard didn't kill anyone."

Ms. Pryce got back in her car. "You better get back home. The police are waiting for you." Her car tore out of the alley, spraying sharp missiles of gravel against my bare legs. Now it would feel good to have that little dog lick my legs again. The dog and the two guys had disappeared.

Now what? It was the Zwake Curse. Uncle Stoppard was being taken to jail. I would be thrown into a foster home. One by one, the members of my family were taken away from me. First my aunt, then my parents, and finally Uncle Stoppard.

The police had to realize that Uncle Stoppard couldn't possibly be the murderer. Why would he kill that stranger? He didn't even know him. Of course, the police might think we were protecting our possessions, that Uncle Stoppard discovered the guy stealing our stuff, and then hit him. But if Uncle Stoppard did kill him, he wouldn't be stupid enough to leave him in his very own storage room. He'd dispose of the body. Uncle Stop is smart enough to figure out all kinds of ways of killing people. Just look at his books. He understands all about clues and evidence and fingerprints. Don't the police read?

Still, it would take time. It might be days, or even weeks, before they proved that Uncle Stoppard was innocent. Where would I stay during that time? A foster home? A jail cell? A prison camp up in the north woods with older boys who stole cars and sold drugs?

At the back of our building there's an old metal downspout. Just underneath, where the water gushes out onto the grass, is a large, flat stone. Uncle Stoppard says the stone keeps the water from eroding a hole in the soil. Under the stone is an extra key to our back door. Uncle Stoppard and I keep it there for emergencies, such as getting locked out of our apartment. This was an emergency.

If I rode back to the apartment now, the police would nab me. I decided to wait, hidden in the lilac bushes. I don't know how long I stood there. Then I walked my bike quietly back up the alley. The lights were out in our apartment. I leaned the bike against the darker, back side of the building, and crept toward the front. No police cars, but the front yard was covered with old flashbulbs. The grass was flattened from lots of people's shoes. A police barricade, a bright orange-striped sawhorse, blocked the entrance to the apartment building's main door. What if the police returned? If they saw my bike, they would know I was here.

Walking toward the back of the building, a light caught my eye. It was a reflection. Partly hidden behind a lilac bush, one of our basement windows reflected a light from the building next door. Funny. Only one of our windows caught the light. I looked closer and noticed the window was unlocked, it was tilted slightly outward, less than an inch, just enough to catch the light. Is this how the burglar got into the basement? The police must have seen this. They must realize that Uncle Stoppard wouldn't crawl through a basement window when he could simply walk down the stairs.

I fetched the apartment key from under the waterspout stone. Once inside the back door, I automatically activated the security light. Rats! I scurried up the stairs to our back door, opened it, and slipped inside. I didn't turn on the light in the kitchen in case the apartment was being spied on by the police. I groped my way to my bedroom, found my bedside table, and opened the top drawer. The aluminum key for my bike lock felt cool to my groping fingers. Back outside, I got on my bike and rode over to an all-night pop machine I saw earlier while hunting for the burglar chick. I locked my bike to a weird pipe contraption that stood next to the machine. This way the police wouldn't see my bike at our building and might think I rode away. I walked back to the apartment. I made sure to stay in the shadows in case the police drove by. Once I thought I saw Ms. Pryce's big car glide by, so I flattened myself against the side of a house. A thick soapy smell of a clothes dryer hung in the air. Someone was doing his or her laundry. The big car passed by, and I slunk back home.

Inside the dark apartment I was finally able to breathe. I felt as if I had been holding my breath underwater for ten hours. Should I call the police station and ask about Uncle Stoppard, and find out where he was being kept? Better not. The police might trace the call. They'd know I was home.

I was dying for a nice cold can of pop, but I was afraid of opening the refrigerator door and lighting up the kitchen. The microwave clock glowed 11:45. I think Sergeant Linker had knocked at our front door around eight o'clock. That means I must have been outside for more than two hours. I walked toward my bedroom, then stopped. If the police do come back, that's the first place they would look. Safer to sleep in Uncle Stoppard's room. I made a bundle of pillows and clothes in my bed and covered it with the bedspread, so that if someone glanced in, they'd think I was sleeping in there; I saw that trick on television. Then I went to Uncle Stop's room.

I heard footsteps in the back hallway. The security light gleamed through the narrow blinds in the kitchen window. I held my breath. Two sets of footsteps. I didn't dare move the blinds to see who it was. The feet walked past our back door and turned. They headed upstairs. It must be the nurses. Then I heard Joan's voice, sounding quiet and nervous. "Technically, you're right," she said. "It's not stealing if it belongs to you in the first place," said Alison. "We'll call them in the morning." Was that Joan again? The footsteps and voices vanished up the stairs.

Where did they come from? Had they been in the basement? I remembered the open window. When the police had come earlier that evening it had still been light outdoors. They might not have noticed that basement window leaning slightly open. I only saw it because of the light from next door, but that light wouldn't have been on when the police were here. Should I call them or not? Maybe I should go see if there are any important clues lying down there. I could call the police in the morning from a pay phone, so they couldn't trace the call to the apartment.

I grabbed the flashlight we keep in the kitchen. Downstairs, I found more police tape crisscrossing the entrance of our storage room like a plastic yellow spiderweb. I thought I heard tiny scratching sounds in the dark corners of the basement. Rats. Too bad Pablo's body was discovered before the furry guys could have another picnic. Where was Pablo anyway? Ms. Pryce said he hadn't been killed. Was he sitting comfortably upstairs in his apartment, laughing over his new golden goodies hidden away in some closet, or was he lying on a comfy hospital bed somewhere, scheming to nab the rest of the Zwake treasure?

Why would someone attack Pablo? He was the burglar. Maybe he was working with someone else, an accomplice. A female accomplice! The woman that Ms. Pryce saw run out the back door. Maybe Pablo and Miss Bikeathon had an argument over their loot. She grabbed the ski pole, stabbed him in the back, and then escaped with—hmm, with what? More of my gold from Agualar? It wouldn't be easy carrying

Mayan artifacts on a bike. Gold might be soft, but it was heavy. You needed a car to haul the stuff around.

A spooky flashlight beam bounced above the wooden basement steps. Someone else was coming downstairs. I slipped behind the washing machines. They smelled wet and moldy. Kneeling down, I switched off my flashlight.

A dark figure walked toward the storage rooms. Hard shoes squeaked across the cold cement floor. It was Mr. Barrymore. He flashed his light at each one of the storage rooms. Carefully he checked the locks on each door. He stood for a few minutes without moving, then walked back toward the washing machines. I tried making myself as small as I could. I backed away from Mr. Barrymore and his searching beam. I hoped I wouldn't back up into a hungry, beady-eyed, whisker-twitching rodent.

Mr. Barrymore was searching for something. He spent fifteen more minutes sneaking around the room, spraying his flashlight beam along the walls. I heard him make a satisfied "Hmmmph" sound. His footsteps creaked up the stairs. I stayed crouched in the darkness until I heard the faraway sound of his back door shutting behind him.

6
Cracks and Crooks

I fell asleep on the basement floor. The last thing I remembered was Mr. Barrymore's door shutting, then I blinked and I was lying on my back. I don't know how long I had been lying there, I just knew I was cold and tired. I found my flashlight, switched it on, and headed upstairs.

I could tell it was still dark outside. When I got to the kitchen, the microwave clock showed 3:18. Well, at least the police didn't come back. I set the flashlight on the kitchen table and tiptoed toward Uncle Stoppard's room. I felt my way through the dark, and eventually felt the edge of his bed. I pulled off my shoes and socks and jumped onto the mattress.

Then I heard the third scream of that night. It was Uncle Stoppard again.

"Who the—Finnegan, is that you?"

"Uncle Stoppard, you're not in jail!"

"Of course not."

"But Ms. Pryce said you were the murderer."

Uncle Stoppard switched on the lamp next to his bed. His wavy reddish hair stood up in spikes all over his head. His cucumber-green eyes looked pickled. A thin gold chain around his neck gleamed in the light.

"Turn it off!" I said.

"Why?"

"The police will see it."

"They know I'm here, Finn. They released me."

"But Ms. Pryce said—"

Uncle Stoppard reached for a hankie from beneath his pillow. "Ms. Pryce is a pain in the butt sometimes." He blew his nose with a loud honk.

I moved in closer to him. "Do the police think you tried to kill Pablo?"

"Oh, so you know he's not dead?"

"Ms. Pryce told me."

"Our landlady is a geyser of information." Uncle Stoppard put his hand on my knee. "No, thankfully Pablo isn't dead. He's got a punctured lung, though. They took him to St. Mary's Hospital."

"But what happened? With you, I mean."

"The police took me in for questioning. And I'm still under suspicion."

"But—"

"Just like everyone else in the building."

"But you couldn't have done it."

"It was my storage room," said Uncle Stoppard. "My property. I could have been protecting the gold when I killed—"

"But you were in the apartment all day Sunday."

"The police think the murder took place on Friday."

Friday. That's before Pablo left for his computer convention. "We went to a movie on Friday. Didn't you tell the police that?"

Uncle Stoppard had a funny look in his eye. Was he just tired? "I could have snuck down to the storage room after you fell asleep that night. Or perhaps I hid the body right before we left for the movies."

I didn't like where this conversation was going. "No one could sit through a movie and eat popcorn after they killed a guy."

Uncle Stoppard shrugged. "Some people don't feel anything when they take a human life. Especially if they have killed before." Then he added: "Especially if the movie and the popcorn are really good."

"Uncle Stoppard!"

"I'm joking."

"So why'd they let you go?" I asked.

"They figure I'm not the kind of guy to skip town. But I'm sure they'll keep an eye on me. What time is it?" He grabbed his glasses from the bedside table, put them on, and looked at his clock. "I guess I was down there a couple hours. When I got back, I saw you asleep and didn't want to wake you."

That trick from TV really works.

"Did Ms. Pryce let you back in the apartment?" he asked.

I shook my head. "I used the key under the stone."

"Ah, I forgot about that."

"So what happened at the station?"

"While we were still in the apartment, I explained that I had hurt my foot in the hallway. The police questioned the two nurses upstairs after you ran out the back. Do you realize how dangerous it was for you to ride off like that?"

"But I couldn't let the burglar get away."

"Yeah, the police said how Ms. Pryce told them a strange woman ran past her out of Pablo's apartment and out the back door."

"Did she say what the burglar looked like?"

"All Ms. Pryce remembered was long, dark hair. I don't think they found her, yet. And we don't even know if the woman was the burglar or not."

"Of course she's the burglar. Why else was she running?"

"Maybe she's a friend of Pablo. Maybe she was running after the real burglar."

"Well, Pablo can tell us who the burglar is."

"Pablo was stabbed in the back, remember? He may not even have seen who attacked him."

I told Uncle Stoppard my idea of what happened, about Pablo and his accomplice arguing about their loot. "That's an interesting theory," he said.

"Or maybe Pablo told his friend to stab him on purpose," I said. "That way he could call the police and tell them he had been attacked by a burglar. And the police would think someone else besides Pablo was stealing all our gold."

Uncle Stoppard smiled. "You should help me write my next mystery, Finn."

"You don't think it could happen like that?" I asked.

"It could. But I don't think someone would want to get a punctured lung on purpose."

"It was an accident," I said. "Pablo's girlfriend just stabbed him a little too hard, that's all."

"His girlfriend?"

"She should have been more careful. That ski pole is really sharp."

"You're telling me."

"I'll bet it could even go through wood," I said.

"Funny you should say that, Finn. That's what the police think happened."

I felt cold again. "What, uh, what do they think?"

"Come here." Uncle Stoppard climbed out of bed and walked into the hallway. "Let's see, where is that? Oh, yes." I noticed now that the bookcase had been moved again, this time revealing the crack that the ski pole had poked through. A round circle drawn in yellow chalk showed where the umbrella stand had once stood. "Look what the police found."

I didn't have to look. I knew exactly what they found.

"See this crack?" said Uncle Stoppard. "Detective Linker thinks the ski pole had been pushed through here. Pablo and his attacker may have been fighting over both ski poles. One got stuck here—the one I stepped on later. And the other one wound up in Pablo's back."

"What about the blood on the umbrella stand?"

"It must have been blood from the ski pole. The pole probably slipped back down below the crack after I stepped on it, then when you were cleaning up my books, you got some blood from the crack onto the bottom of the stand."

"Interesting theory," I said.

Uncle Stoppard looked at me. "You have another one?"

"Uh, not at the moment."

"With an imagination like yours, I'm sure you'll come up with another one. Well, the cops took the umbrella stand and both poles in for examining."

My stomach flip-flopped. Thanks to that blond Jared guy, the police now had my fingerprints on file.

"Oh, and guess what else?" said Uncle Stoppard.

I was afraid to ask.

"I had to go down to the station to make a statement, and while I was waiting I met Officer Lemon-Olsen."

"That Jared guy?"

"Yeah. He told me they found something weird about the fingerprints." Weird? I followed Uncle Stoppard back into his bedroom, where we sat back down on the bed. "The only fingerprints on the lock to our storage room were yours and mine."

"That isn't so weird."

"But there should have been someone else's fingerprints on the lock, too—Pablo's."

"Because Pablo's the thief, right?"

"Because Pablo told us he replaced the old lock before he flew to Seattle for his convention. Unless he was wearing gloves—and why would he?—his prints should have been on the new lock."

"Someone wiped them off," I said.

"Exactly," Uncle Stoppard said. "Which tells us someone was tampering with the storage room since Pablo put on the lock. Since last Friday."

Friday again.

"The police also found out who the dead man is. Was."

"Who?"

"Pablo's friend Larry."

The guy who was supposed to water Pablo's plants and collect Pablo's mail and give the landlady Pablo's rent check. That's why Pablo's mail was still sitting in the hall, and why Ms. Pryce entered his apartment, angry about the rent being late.

"But the police don't know why Larry was down there in the first place," Uncle Stoppard added.

"Pablo's the head of a burglar ring," I said. "He and his friend Larry and a girlfriend all work together. Then the girlfriend got greedy, so she killed Larry first. Then she tried to get rid of Pablo."

"I don't think so," said Uncle Stoppard.

"Why not? That kind of thing happens all the time on crime shows."

"Jared told me that the police don't have any kind of record for Pablo's friend, Larry. Or for Pablo. And their fingerprints aren't on file. People just don't decide to become superburglars overnight. They've usually been involved in crime since they were young."

"Hey, if that Larry's fingerprints weren't on file, how did the police know who he was?"

"He was wearing some kind of medical bracelet."

"I've got it!" I said. "Pablo became a crook *because* he discovered all that Agualar gold. "He got greedy and it was the first time he ever stole something."

Uncle Stoppard's eyes crinkled up.

"You don't find a treasure in your basement every day," I said.

"Instant wealth is a strong temptation to resist," Uncle Stoppard agreed. "Especially for someone who needs money. And who doesn't need more money?"

"Mona Trafalgar-Squeer?" I suggested.

Uncle Stoppard ignored me. "The most puzzling thing about the murders and the thefts is the timing."

"Timing?"

"Why should it happen now? The gold has been downstairs for seven years. Pablo's been sharing that storage room with us for three years. Why are the artifacts being stolen now?"

"It's the Zwake Curse," I said.

"Maybe," said Uncle Stoppard. "But why should the curse blow up *this* week? Why not last week? Or last year?"

"That's what you mean by timing."

"Yeah."

"Could he have some big bill to pay? Like drugs or blackmail? Pablo could have been digging through our stuff to find something to sell for money and then, lucky for him, he found my Horizontal Man."

"Well—"

"*And* my gold spoon."

"So why did Pablo kill his friend Larry? And what was Larry doing down there in the first place?"

Uncle Stoppard had me stumped.

"Something must have happened," he said. "Something we don't realize, that set off all these events."

"Like what?"

"Something new, Finn. Some kind of change," said Uncle Stoppard. "And I have a feeling it's right under our noses." He pulled out the handkerchief and honked again.

The morning sky turned a paler shade of blue—the same shade as Ms. Pryce's hair. The stars had vanished. The air felt cool through the open bedroom windows. Uncle Stoppard and I were too wired to go to sleep. We decided to have an early breakfast.

I was munching on a slice of toast smothered in chunky peanut butter. Uncle Stoppard had whole wheat toast and blueberry jam. For some reason, both

Uncle Stoppard and I like to eat our toast standing up. Uncle Stop wanders around the apartment, holding a dish under his chin to catch crumbs, while he makes humming noises. I walked into the front room and was staring out at the trees. Down below sat the orange-striped police barricade.

"What's that orange thing for?" I called out to Uncle Stoppard. He was limping down the hallway with his dish and toast.

"It's to warn people to stay out of the building if they don't have any business here."

"I thought it was to keep us inside."

"We had a lot of reporters around here last night. The police don't want people messing up the area and possibly contaminating evidence."

Evidence. That reminded me of the window downstairs and of Mr. Barrymore's nightly prowling. I told Uncle Stoppard what I witnessed in the basement last night.

"You need to be more careful, Finn. Use your brain. What if Mr. Barrymore is the burglar? What would have happened if he caught you spying on him?"

"I don't know. He was looking around, but he wasn't looking real hard. I mean, he could have seen me if he stayed down there longer."

"Please stay out of the basement, Finn."

"All right."

"Promise me you won't go down there again."

"Okay, I promise."

"Good. Now, did you find anything that looked like a clue by the open window?"

"Window?" I stopped chewing my toast. "I was so

surprised by Mr. Barrymore that after he left, I forgot all about the window."

Uncle Stoppard set his dish down. "We better take a look."

He pulled a pair of shorts on over his underwear, grabbed the flashlight off the kitchen table, and headed downstairs. We turned on all the basement lights.

"Whew! What's that smell?" he asked.

"I smelled that last night. You don't think it's another body, do you?"

"Nah, it's different." He sniffed a few times. "It reminds me of a wet dog."

"I saw a really neat dog last night. He licked my knees."

"Your knees?"

"Yeah. It was right after Ms. Pryce almost ran me over in her big new car."

Uncle Stoppard leaned against a washing machine and stared at me. "Would you mind telling me exactly what happened last night after you raced out of here."

"After the scream?"

"Yes. After Ms. Pryce's scream."

As carefully as I could, I told Uncle Stoppard, step by step, what happened after I took my bike outside and raced after the burglar. I told him about the two guys with their cool dog. I mentioned how I heard the two nurses talking in the back hallway.

"But you didn't see them?" he asked.

"No, I didn't want to move the blinds."

Uncle Stoppard made me repeat, word for word, and as best I could, what I heard the roommates say to each other.

"I wonder who they're planning to call this morning?" he said.

Neither Uncle Stoppard nor I saw anything unusual about the open window. Except that it was open. There were no marks around the wood to show that someone had forced their way in. The lock wasn't broken. Neither was the glass. I wondered how the burglar managed to get in this way. The window was partially hidden by a lilac bush, but you'd think the people next door would notice someone sneaking around, someone trying to break into our basement. The buildings were only a few yards apart. Of course, I never noticed much about our neighbors or *their* building.

"If the burglar is skillful enough to open our padlock," said Uncle Stoppard, "you'd think that a door lock wouldn't stop him."

"Or her," I said.

"So, why come through a window when a door is more convenient?"

"Because the window is more hidden?" I said.

"Climbing behind some lilac bushes, though, would attract more attention from outside than simply walking through a door."

"Maybe the open window is a trick. A clue to throw us off," I said. "Since Pablo is the burglar—"

"*If* he's the burglar," said Uncle Stoppard.

"Pablo doesn't have to tamper with our padlock. He's already got a key. You see, Pablo is very clever," I said. "He opened this window to make us, and the police, think that the burglar doesn't live in the building. That it's an outside job."

"An interesting point," said Uncle Stoppard.

Finally, Uncle Stoppard was beginning to see the light. It sometimes takes him a while, but eventually he figures things out.

"About that key," said Uncle Stoppard.

"Key?"

He walked over to our storage room door covered with yellow police tape. I mean, the *door* was covered in tape, not Uncle Stoppard. He stared closely at the shiny new padlock. His green eyes got that serious, squinty look. Then he whipped around and looked at me.

"When Pablo bought this lock, he had a key for himself and one for us."

"That's what he said."

"When you buy a new padlock, it usually comes with several keys in case you lose one. Pablo's friend Larry must also have had a key."

"Why would Larry have one?"

"If Pablo gave him the keys to his apartment to water his plants, maybe Larry also got a copy of the storage room key. Pablo might have handed him a ring with all the keys strung together."

"And whoever killed Larry now has the keys," I said.

"I should ask Jared if the police found any keys on Larry's body," said Uncle Stoppard.

That's how the storage room door was unlocked after I got locked in. Someone used the other key. Does that mean that the killer who locked me inside is the same person who freed me? Which still didn't explain why they locked and then *unlocked* me in that room.

"I wonder if the police have talked with Pablo

about this," said Uncle Stoppard. "We should tell Ms. Pryce so she can change the locks on Pablo's apartment."

"Maybe Larry *was* a burglar," I said, "who just happened to be killed by *another* burglar."

"Two burglars just happened to be burgling the same building at the same time?"

"Yes," I said.

"Too complicated," said Uncle Stoppard.

"You're right. Too Mona."

Uncle Stoppard shot me an icy glance.

"Maybe the burglar knocked Larry out," I said, "and ran down here with the keys. And then Larry woke up, rushed downstairs, and got killed."

"I think someone in Larry's position would call the police first, before he charged after someone who had just knocked him out. Besides, there was no sign of forced entry in any of the apartments."

"How do you know that?"

"Jared told me."

"What if the burglar had a gun?" I said.

"That still doesn't explain—"

"Sure it does. The burglar knocks on Pablo's door, and pulls a gun on Larry."

"Knocks on the door?"

"Then he—or she—forces Larry down here to open the storage room. And once it's opened, bang!"

"There was no bang," said Uncle Stoppard.

I remembered that Ms. Pryce said she had heard a thumping sound in the night coming from next door.

"Want to hear a scary thought?" said Uncle Stoppard.

"No."

"If the burglar forced Larry to come down here, that means the burglar already knew there was gold inside that storage room."

My stomach turned to stone, squeezed into a hard, round ball, and fell into my shoes. Uncle Stoppard was right. The only people who knew about the gold were dead. Really dead (Aunt Verona), legally dead (Mom and Dad), or sometimes brain-dead (me and Uncle Stoppard). Did the Zwake Curse involve ghosts? Our family always did have a fondness for dead things.

"But there is our second theory," said Uncle Stoppard.

Thank goodness for a second theory.

"The burglar broke into the basement, rummaging through the stuff in this big open room first. Larry heard some noises, came down to investigate, and surprised the burglar—"

"I'd say the burglar surprised Larry."

"And Larry's keys conveniently fell into the burglar's lap, so to speak."

"And the lucky burglar found which padlock fitted Larry's keys, and started going through our stuff." That thief was too lucky: finding keys to the one room in the entire apartment building that contained priceless gold artifacts that belonged to me.

"Then Larry's body was dragged inside the room to hide it," said Uncle Stoppard.

I looked at the storage room door. Which reminded me of Dad's diary. Which reminded me of something else. "About that curse," I said. "Did my dad have a lucky hunting knife?"

Uncle Stoppard turned to look at me. "I haven't

thought about that knife for years," he said. "It was a gift from some Indian chief out in Montana. You know, your father was a very brave guy."

"*Is* a brave guy."

"He saved the chief's son from a landslide." Uncle Stop took off his glasses and polished them on his T-shirt. "Leo and Anna were working on a dig out in the Montana Rockies, trying to hunt down some lost treasure of Lewis and Clark's, you know, the explorers who surveyed the land between the Mississippi and the Pacific Ocean? Well, one of your folks' teamworkers was the son of a Blackfoot chief. One night, after work, the boy got trapped by a small landslide on a steep, rocky slope while heading home. The slope ended in a sheer hundred-foot drop. The kid started sliding toward the edge, but luckily Leo heard the kid yelling for help. He climbed out onto another slippery ledge—and it was dark, remember—threw a rope down to the kid, and helped pull him to safety."

"Wow!"

"To show his gratitude, the boy's father gave Leo a hunting knife that was made before the Civil War. I saw it once. The handle was buffalo bone, and the blade was still sharp. Your dad always called it his lucky knife. When your folks came back from Agualar, Leo told me how all their bad luck began when that knife disappeared."

Lucky knife. Lucky burglar. Unlucky Dad.

Uncle Stoppard sniffed the air. "Boy, that smell really is putrid." He walked around, following the scent like a dog after a french fry. Soon Uncle Stoppard was on his knees by the washing machines. He was crouching in the same spot where I hid from Mr. Barrymore last night. "Aha!" he cried. "This is it."

"The smell?" I asked. Uncle Stoppard stood up, threw open one of the machine lids, and an odor of mildewed clothes swarmed into our nostrils. Someone had forgotten to take his clothes out of the machine and dry them.

"This is what killed Larry," said Uncle Stoppard.

"They stuck him in the washing machine?"

"He was washing clothes the night he was killed. He came down here after the machine stopped, saw the storage room door open, surprised the burglar, and bang!"

"You said there was no bang."

"Okay, then. Bong! He was hit over the head and killed."

"How do you know those aren't Pablo's?" I asked.

Uncle Stoppard lifted some white shorts. "These are Montgomery Wards. Pablo is strictly a Calvin Klein or Versace guy."

"How do you know that?"

"Writers are keen observers of life, Finnegan. And look, the whites are mixed with the colors. Pablo's too organized for that."

The colored clothes were blue, red, black, and gray. Not Mr. Barrymore's Munchkin colors, either.

Uncle Stoppard's guess made the most sense of anything so far. It made me feel even worse for poor Larry, though. I never met him, but I had to feel sorry for him. The guy was dead just because he wanted clean underwear.

7
Who Lied?

We trudged upstairs and tried sleeping for a few hours. All I remember was dissecting the fake "sleeping Finn," pulling apart the bundle of clothes and pillows that was supposed to fool the police but fooled Uncle Stoppard instead. Next thing I know, it's a few hours later and Uncle Stoppard is banging around in the kitchen making breakfast. Or was it brunch?

Something was wrong. I sat up and stared at the top of my dresser.

"Uncle Stoppard!" Now it was my turn to yell.

Uncle Stoppard stuck his head inside my door, a glass of orange juice in one hand and a metal spatula in the other. "And good morning to you, too, Finn."

"The photo is gone."

"What?"

I jumped out of bed and stood next to my dresser. "Look, the photo is gone. The picture of me and my parents and the Horizontal Man."

"The photo from Agualar?"

"And my gold coin!"

"Search the floor."

We searched the entire bedroom. I opened all the drawers and pulled out clothes, socks, and comic books, thinking that maybe the picture had slipped off the dresser and landed in an open drawer. No picture. And the coin couldn't possibly have fallen off because there's a little wooden rail that runs around the top of the dresser. Somebody nabbed it.

We looked under the bed. We looked under the rug under the bed. We even looked under the dust under the rug under the bed. Uncle Stoppard started rummaging through the rest of the apartment.

Wa-aa-aa-aa-aa-aa-aa-aa-aa!!

The smoke alarm shrieked at us from our hall ceiling.

"The waffles are burning!" I yelled. "I mean, the bacon!"

Uncle Stoppard ran back into the kitchen and grabbed a chair, pulling it into the hall next to the bookcase. He jumped up on the chair and reached for the smoke detector.

"How does this thing work?" he yelled.

I threw open the back door for some fresh air. Using one of Uncle Stoppard's cookbooks as a fan, I tried waving the smoke into the back hallway and away from the detector.

"Should I push this little blue button?" Uncle Stoppard yelled.

"Go ahead," I yelled back.

In the back hallway, I saw people walking down from the floor above. Two police officers I had never seen before. Wow, they're quick, I thought.

"That's not it," yelled Uncle Stoppard.

"What?" I said.

"The blue button didn't work!"

Behind the police officers came Joan and Alison.

All four people stared at me as I stood in the doorway, fanning thick clouds of greasy smoke from the kitchen.

"Finnegan!" exclaimed Joan.

"Are you all right, son?" asked a uniform.

"It's just breakfast," I explained.

"What?" yelled Uncle Stoppard from the hall.

"The police are here," I shouted.

"Please hear what?" asked Uncle Stoppard.

The alarm shut off. "The police—" I shouted. "Oh, sorry."

Uncle Stoppard joined me at the doorway. "What's going on, Finn?"

Joan walked over to us as Alison and the two cops started down the stairs. "It's Alison's bike," she said. "The burglar must have taken it last night."

"My picture was stolen, too," I said. I didn't mention my gold coin. I didn't want anyone to know there was more treasure in our apartment.

"Picture?" she said.

I described the photo to Joan. Her eyes grew wide. "It sounds like one of your mysteries, Mr. Sterling. A mysterious thief steals a photo for some weird, unknown reason."

"We still don't know if it's actually stolen or not," said Uncle Stoppard. "We may have just misplaced it."

"That photo is always on my dresser," I said.

"Always?" he asked.

"Yes."

"Remember when you showed the photo to me the other day?" he said. "You were telling me about the Horizontal Man you saw in Pablo's apartment?"

"Was Pablo having another one of his parties?" asked Joan.

I remembered showing Uncle Stoppard the photo. I had pulled it off the dresser and handed it to him in his office.

"Did you put the photo back?" he asked.

"Of course I did. I mean, um, I'm sure I did."

"We'll look in the office," said Uncle Stoppard. Then he looked at Joan. "Sorry about your roommate's bike."

She shrugged her shoulders. "Yeah, thanks. Hopefully her insurance will cover it. It was a very expensive bike." Joan disappeared down the steps to join her friend.

"I want my picture back," I said.

Uncle Stoppard handed me a loaf of bread that he pulled from the refrigerator. "Start making toast. I'll go look in my office some more."

"Look for the coin, too," I reminded him.

By the time I had loaded a plate with four buttered slices, Uncle Stoppard returned to the kitchen. He shook his head. "Sorry, Finn, I couldn't find it."

"You didn't look hard enough."

"It's not in there, Finn."

"Let's go tell those two cops downstairs."

"Are you sure you put it back on the dresser?"

"Yes, I'm sure."

"Let's look one more time before we call the police."

An hour later, Uncle Stoppard and I were sitting in the kitchen again. The two uniforms had driven away, Joan and Alison were back in their apartment, and the photo of my parents, the only one I had in the entire universe, was another victim of the famous family curse.

"Why would someone want your photo?" asked Uncle Stoppard.

"Greed," I said. "The burglar wants all my gold even if it's just a picture of it."

"The more important question," said Uncle Stoppard, "is *when* did the thief take it."

When was my bedroom unguarded?

"Last night," I said. The apartment had been empty for several hours. With Uncle Stoppard at the police station and me riding around the neighborhood, a whole band of thieves could have walked right in and snatched the refrigerator if they had wanted.

No, the apartment was empty earlier than that. When I was trapped in the storage room. "That's why someone locked me in the room downstairs," I said. "To search our apartment for more gold and steal my photo."

"The burglar would be taking an awful chance coming back into the apartment," said Uncle Stoppard. "Especially since the police had been in and out."

Unless the burglar was still in the building and had never left at all. Maybe Uncle Stoppard and I were each half-right about the strange woman who ran out of Pablo's apartment and passed Ms. Pryce. The woman could have been a friend of Pablo (Uncle Stoppard's idea). She may have seen a burglar attack Pablo, ran upstairs to dial 911, and then panicked, afraid that the killer burglar (my idea) might come after her, too. Running away made her look suspicious, but we don't really know if the woman was the burglar. And if she was not the burglar, the real burglar could have been hiding in the building. Or *living* in the building.

"I think I'll call Jared and ask him whether this is a police matter," said Uncle Stoppard.

Last night, at the moment Ms. Pryce screamed in the back hallway, Pablo was lying unconscious in the basement. Joan and Alison were in their apartment, after helping Uncle Stoppard with his foot. But where was Mr. Barrymore? Why hadn't we seen him? With all the yelling and running and hundreds of cops and thousands of reporters on the front lawn, a normal person would have stuck his head out of his apartment and asked what was going on.

"Where was Mr. Barrymore last night?" I asked.

Uncle Stoppard was now sitting next to the phone in the living room, paging through his book of phone numbers. "Barrymore? In his apartment, I guess. Why?"

"Just wondering."

"Poor guy is so shy. I wonder if he ever got his kilt clean?"

While Uncle Stoppard dialed the phone I quietly slipped out the kitchen door and walked up to the third floor. I didn't know if Mr. Barrymore was even home, but it was still morning. He might be finishing breakfast, or brushing his teeth, getting ready for work.

After the fourth knock, Mr. Barrymore's back door opened slowly. It stopped short, attached to a small chain. I could see part of Mr. Barrymore's face peering at me through the narrow opening.

"Uh, Mr. Barrymore—" I began.

He didn't say a word. I could see a slice of orange

pants and a green shirt. More Munchkin colors. His left eyebrow, moving like a slow, brown caterpillar, stretched up toward his forehead.

"Mr. Barrymore?" I said.

"I heard you the first time."

I didn't know what I was going to say. "Uh, did you lose something?"

He stared at me with a weird light in his eye. "Lose something?"

"Um, yes. I was downstairs last night, and I just wondered—"

"She's lying," he whispered.

"What?"

"Lying," he whispered louder. "She is lying."

"Who's lying?"

"Don't bother me anymore."

"Who's she?" I asked. "You mean Ms. Pryce?"

"I already told you—" His eye looked over my head, then the door slammed shut.

I turned around and saw Joan coming out of her apartment. "Finnegan," she said. "Is your uncle still home?"

"Uh, yeah."

"Terrific. I have a little favor to ask him." She looked at Mr. Barrymore's closed door. "I'm sorry, did I interrupt something?"

"No. Nothing."

When we reached our apartment, Joan held a book out to Uncle Stoppard. "Would you do me the honor of autographing *Cold Feet* for me?"

"Sure," he said, smiling. "Finnegan, hand me that pen."

"How's your foot this morning?"

"Just fine, thanks."

"You know, Mr. Sterling," said Joan. "You are one of my top favorite authors of all time."

"Is that so?" said Uncle Stoppard.

"Oh, yes."

"You read a lot then?"

"All the time," she said. "Right now I'm finishing up *Castaways* by Mona Trafalgar-Squeer. Ever read it?"

"No."

I raised my hand. "I have."

"Isn't it terrific?" said Joan. "This is the third time I've read it. Where does she come up with her ideas? And that pygmy detective. Pretty original, I'd say."

"Real original," I said.

"You know," said Joan. "I once saw her downtown driving that huge silver motorcycle of hers. I wonder how much she paid for that monster."

"It defies imagination," said Uncle Stoppard.

"I'll say. I guess that's why you two are writers," said Joan. "Imagination. Thanks so much for the autograph." Joan stared at Uncle Stoppard's signature on the inside front cover. "Well, I gotta be going. Bye."

"Bye," I said.

Uncle Stoppard dropped on the couch. "I spoke with Jared on the phone. He thinks your missing photo could be important."

"Of course it's important! It's extremely important."

"He means important to the investigation. Each item stolen gives us another clue to the mind of the murderer. He also said we should check the apartment to see if anything else is missing."

I ran back to the kitchen and yanked open the silverware drawer. The golden spoon was gone! Then I remembered that the police had taken it away in an evidence bag.

"I also told Jared about the stolen bike," said Uncle Stoppard.

Too bad I didn't get close enough to the burglar, or accomplice, or whatever she's called, while I was chasing her last night. I could have identified the bike for the police and they'd realize that Uncle Stoppard wasn't the burglar. And I'd get my photo back. It could be resting safely on top of my dresser right now.

"By the way," said Uncle Stoppard. "Where were you when I was on the phone with Jared?"

"Oh, just standing out back," I lied. "Looking out the windows. I was wondering if it was going to rain."

"Looks nice and sunny out to me," said Uncle Stoppard.

Mr. Barrymore's face popped into my mind. His one brown eyeball beneath the hairy caterpillar of an eyebrow stared at me again. Half of his mouth whispered the words, "Lying. She's lying."

She. There were the only three "she's" in the whole building: Ms. Pryce, Joan, and Alison. Detective Linker was a "she," too, but she didn't actually count. Mr. Barrymore must have meant one of his three neighbors. But which one?

The afternoon stayed bright and sunny so Uncle Stoppard and I walked to Uptown, which was only six blocks away. Uptown is this cool part of town right next to three of the biggest, bluest lakes in Minneapolis. Lots of young people like me, or old people like Uncle Stoppard, hang out there watching other peo-

THE HORIZONTAL MAN   107

ple: boarders; bikers; skaters; joggers; dog-walkers; teenagers with metal balls in their tongues and tattoos on their necks asking for spare change; pretty girls and handsome guys eating fancy food outdoors on tiny metal tables. Uncle Stoppard goes to Uptown a lot because of the library. The library is underground, and the only other one like it in the whole country is in New York City. Today we walked to Uptown because Uncle Stoppard said we needed to get out of the house and fill our lungs with fresh air. Fresh, noisy air, with pickups and motorcycles whizzing by, car radios pumping out music, delivery trucks beeping. Those restaurant customers at the outdoor tables sometimes had to shout because of the traffic.

We also walked to Uptown because we were going to meet Jared Lemon-Olsen (the fingerprint expert) for coffee. Uptown must have a hundred different coffee shops, but they all serve the same kind of coffee. Beans are beans. The only thing different about each shop was the type of crowd that hung out there. If you liked to laugh real loud, joke with your friends, needed a place to rest after skating around the lakes, and didn't care how you were dressed, or if your hair was messy, you hung out at Cafe Olé. Pink and blue bulls and matadors in gold suits waving red capes decorated the walls. A few dusty cactus plants slumped in the windows. An old stereo speaker hung outside over the door and played Mexican, I mean, Hispanic tunes. Uncle Stoppard said it was called "mariachi music." Whenever I sat on one of Cafe Olé's wooden benches in the hot sun and closed my eyes, I could pretend I was in Agualar.

As soon as we walked by the Drinkin' Incan coffee

shop and crossed the street to Cafe Olé, we saw Jared
sitting at one of the outdoor benches that had a table.
He waved and we waved back.

"Where's your uniform?" I said.

Jared laughed. "Today's my day off." He wore
jeans, orange work boots, and a yellow T-shirt that
matched his sideburns and mustache. He wore glasses,
too. "My contacts were bothering me," he explained.

He and Uncle Stoppard drank cups of Mad Matador
Mocha. I drank raspberry pop. While the two of them
talked about Pablo and Dead Larry, I pulled my father's journal out of my backpack. I brought it with
me for a couple reasons. First, I wanted to finish reading it, and I figured it might be more interesting in
case Uncle Stoppard and Jared started talking about
boring grown-up stuff. Second, there were some blank
pages at the end of the journal and I needed to make
notes. So much had happened in the last few days that
it was hard to keep track of it all. I made a list.

The Mystery of the Horizontal Man

Baffling Questions

Why was Larry killed?

What happened to Larry's (Pablo's) keys?

Why was the Horizontal Man on Pablo's table?

Why was the spoon in the dish rack?

How did the burglar get into the building?
    (open window?)

Are the burglar and the killer the same person?

Stolen items (that we know of): *photo!!!,* statue,
    coin, Alison's bike

Who was the woman running out of Pablo's
    apartment?
What kind of jerk would steal a photo?
Who was the "she" who lied (according to Mr.
    Barrymore)?
What was Mr. Barrymore looking for in the
    basement?
When did the burglar steal the Agualar photo
    and why?

I figured I knew the answer to this question already.
The photo must have been stolen while I was trapped
in the storage room. And the reason it was stolen:
pure, stupid meanness.

Uncle Stoppard's Questions

Why is all this happening now?
What big change, or event, occurred that started
    all the trouble?

"Do you hate it when people ask for your autograph?" I heard Jared say out of the corner of my ear.

"Not at all," said Uncle Stoppard.

"Good." Jared dug into a green nylon backpack
laying on the sidewalk next to the bench. He pulled
out a worn copy of *Cold Feet* and a felt-tip pen and
threw them both on the wooden table. "Would you
mind?" he asked.

Uncle Stoppard grinned and flipped the book over.

"I was afraid to ask," said Jared. "You could say I,
uh, had cold feet."

I think Uncle Stoppard and I have heard that joke a million times.

"That's one I haven't heard before," said Uncle Stoppard. He handed the book back to Jared.

"So where was this photo taken?" asked Jared.

"It was taken right off my dresser," I said.

"He's talking about the photo in the book," said Uncle Stoppard. *"My* photo." He looked at Jared. "It was taken in our front room."

"I took the picture," I said.

"Good job," said Jared. "It's a lot clearer than some of the shots taken by our crime lab guys."

"If I had known how talented Finn was," said Uncle Stoppard, "I could have had pictures on my other books, too."

"What's that in the background?"

Uncle Stoppard squinted at the photo. "Oh, that's the porch on the building next door."

"Those buildings are really close together," said Jared.

"That's why we don't have a dog," I said. "Uncle Stoppard says we need a real yard."

"I agree," said Jared. "Dogs need lots of space. Hey, did I tell you we found prints on that gold spoon taken from your kitchen?"

"Pablo's prints?" I asked.

Jared nodded. "And yours and your uncle's."

"Doesn't that prove Pablo stole it?" I said.

"No, but it's a good sign," said Jared.

Uncle Stoppard set down his cup of coffee. "There were no other prints found on it?"

"Nope," said Jared.

"Why don't the police arrest Pablo right now?" I asked.

"He's not going anywhere, dude," said Jared. "And there's an officer at the hospital keeping an eye on him."

Good. The officer needs to keep both eyes on that thief.

"It's possible," said Uncle Stoppard, "that the real burglar wore gloves. Just as they did when handling the padlock in the basement."

"We thought of that," said Jared. "And this DeSoto guy doesn't have a previous criminal record, either."

"You mean, he doesn't have a record here in Minnesota," I said.

"Or anywhere in the country. Our computers are plugged into a big national network and into the FBI. If the person who left prints on the spoon was involved in any kind of criminal activity anywhere in the country, we'd know about it."

At another table, some guy with five metal studs in his ear stood up and danced to the mariachi music. His friends laughed at him.

"What if the crook came from another country?" I asked.

"We'd know that, too," said Jared. "But that takes a little longer."

Uncle Stoppard banged his knee against the table and almost spilled all our drinks. "Sorry, uh, how long do prints stay on an object anyway?"

"That depends on the kind of object," said Jared. "The temperature and so forth."

"Could you get prints from someone who had touched something years ago?"

"Years? Well, sure, but—"

"What if the object was gold? And what if it had been sealed up in bubble wrap, and then kept in a cool basement for seven years?"

Jared scratched his yellow mustache. "I guess it's possible. Archeologists have taken prints off of objects thousands of years old."

"My parents are archeologists," I said.

"That's what your uncle told me," said Jared. "But, Stoppard, why is it so important to know about old fingerprints? Cooking up another bestseller?"

"Just curious. I wondered if prints from Finn's parents would still be on it."

"We don't have the equipment to trace something that old. Besides, we don't have the Zwakes' fingerprints on file."

"Yeah, they weren't crooks," I said.

Jared took another sip of coffee. "With no sign of break-ins and very little disturbance in the area, it looks more like an inside job."

"Burglars are pros at breaking in," I said.

"So are archeologists," Jared said, grinning.

"Technically speaking," I said, "archeologists do not steal. They investigate. And they always get permission before they start digging or exploring." Jared stopped grinning.

"You used a chisel and hammer to get into your storage room, didn't you?" he said.

"Not a chisel," said Uncle Stoppard. "A screwdriver."

"Maybe the burglar did the same thing."

"Too noisy," said Uncle Stoppard. "We would have heard something."

"What if you weren't home?" Jared asked.

"Ms. Pryce would have heard it," I said. "She lives on the bottom floor."

"What if she was gone, too?" said Jared. "Or what if she heard the noise and thought it was something else and ignored it?"

"She told the police she didn't hear anything unusual," said Uncle Stoppard.

"What if she lied?" said Jared.

What if she lied? Those were Mr. Barrymore's words: "She's lying." What if Ms. Pryce was the liar he was talking about? Ms. Pryce would be the ideal burglar. She had keys to the apartment building. She was always around. Nobody would think it was strange if they saw her in someone else's apartment. She could say she was checking for rats, or leaving a note, just like when I found her in Pablo's living room.

Could Ms. Pryce have nabbed the Horizontal Man after I left Pablo's apartment?

"Remember the burglar chick on the bicycle?" I said.

"The one who escaped?" said Jared.

"Finnegan chased after her that night on his bike," said Uncle Stoppard.

Jared shook his head. "Pretty bold, dude."

"Pretty dangerous," said Uncle Stoppard.

"There was no burglar," I said.

"What?"

"Ms. Pryce told us about the woman who ran past her," I said. "But no one else saw her."

Uncle Stoppard gave me his cucumber-squint. "You told me you saw a woman on a bicycle on the street that night."

"She could have just been some lady out riding,"
I said.

"And the burglar?" asked Jared.

"No one else saw the strange woman leave the
building. Maybe it was another fake clue."

"Like the open window," said Uncle Stoppard.

"Maybe Ms. Pryce is the burglar and she lied."

8
The Curse Continues

"You need proof," said Jared, sipping more Mad Matador Mocha.

"Proof?" I said. "She's the landlady."

"So?"

"So? She's got keys to all the apartments!"

"Wait a minute, Finn," said Uncle Stoppard. "Remember Larry's keys? The burglar could be using those to get into the storage room."

"You mean the dead guy's keys, right?" said Jared. "They found apartment keys in his pocket. They already returned them to the landlady."

"That's what I mean," I said. "Ms. Pryce is home all the time. She knows when people leave and when they come back. She can tell when someone goes to the basement and puts their stuff into storage. I'll bet she even drilled a peephole into the wall so she could watch the basement whenever she wants."

"Find the hole," said Jared.

"What?"

"Find the hole and show it to the police. They won't listen to your ideas unless they have some kind of evidence."

"Sorry, Finn," said Uncle Stoppard. "But I think Jared is right."

I thought so, too. Even the cops in Uncle Stoppard's books always needed hard evidence. Unfortunately, the real police already had evidence and it was all against Uncle Stoppard. Fingerprints, blood, keys to the site of the murder. Uncle Stoppard even had a motive: to protect his stuff from intruders.

Uncle Stoppard and Jared started talking about other things. Like jogging and fishing. For some reason, Uncle Stop got real excited when Jared was describing different kinds of rods and reels. Don't ask me why. I took a swig of raspberry pop and made a second list.

The Mystery of the Horizontal Man

Suspects and Questions

Ms. Pryce
Pablo
Joan
Alison
Mr. Barrymore
Larry?
Running Woman?

Why steal Agualar treasure? (money)
Who needs money? (everyone)

I wonder where you could trade in a golden Horizontal Man for cash? A pawn shop? An antique store? Someone who likes gold or Maya artifacts? Maybe a museum, like the Ackerberg Institute. It certainly wouldn't be easy to sell.

If Pablo put the new padlock on our storage room on Friday, and if that was the day poor Larry got killed while washing his underwear, I should find out where everyone in the building was on that day. When we get home, I decided, I'll just start at the bottom and work my way up. First on my list, Ms. V. Pryce. I wonder what the V stands for?

"C'mon, Finn, let's go," said Uncle Stoppard, excitedly.

"Already? Hey, where's Jared?"

"He just left. C'mon, we have to meet him back at the house."

"Our house? Why doesn't he come with us?"

"He drove here."

"So why doesn't he drive us home?"

"I'll explain later."

"Does this have something to do with the finger-prints on the spoon?" I asked.

"No," said Uncle Stoppard. "It has to do with fishing."

We had only been back in the apartment for about two minutes, when Jared buzzed at the door. He walked in carrying a big fishing rod and an aluminum tackle box.

"That's just great," said Uncle Stoppard. "Let's go outside."

Fishing sounded boring to me, so I went back to my room and opened up Dad's journal. I found the page where I had left off reading a few days before.

April 7

Work on the dig continues as normal. As normal as possible under the circumstances. Still no sign or word of Verona anywhere. So much has happened in the last weeks. Like any good scientist, I decided to make a careful list of everything that has happened so far, to help me keep track of things.

Dad would like my list. I was behaving just like a scientist. An archeologist.

My first list was to include everyone with a motive for stealing the Horizontal Man. Then I realized my list would fill the rest of my journal. Even though our expedition had been granted permission by the Agualaran authorities, including the Department of National Resources, many locals did not like us disturbing the peace of their ancestors. Several weeks ago, Antonio had told Anna and Verona and I that people living today in Agualar believe that they are the children of the long-dead Maya. They also believe that any Maya artifacts we may discover or dig up actually belong to them.

Poor Dad had a lot more suspects than just five neighbors, a dead guy, and an imaginary running lady.

My second list, the names of the people who had access to the treasure, would also have expanded to book length. Since the artifacts are housed in a trailer near the center of the camp, anyone on the team could have unlocked the door, slipped a

*statue or bowl into their knapsack, and then
walked out again without ever looking suspicious.*

*All we can do now is put tighter controls around
our existing treasure. The trailer is not exactly max-
imum-security. Anna suggested we limit the number of people who can have keys. I know this will
not be a popular suggestion.*

Dad had problems with keys, too.

Uncle Stoppard walked back into the apartment and
changed his sneakers for hiking boots. Then he disappeared up the back stairs. Up? Was he going to talk to
the nurses or Mr. Barrymore? A minute later he came
back down, and marched swiftly through the hall again.
I think he was buzzed from all the Mad Matadors.

"So Mona thinks she's got a monopoly on dwarfs,
eh?" he muttered.

"Mona's detective is a pygmy," I said.

"Yeah?" said Uncle Stoppard. "Well, I got a
midget." He disappeared out the front door. Where
was Jared and his fishing rod?

I turned back to read some more.

April 10–12

*I believe I may have a plan for catching our
thief. Anna, Tomas, and I have spread a rumor—
that another Horizontal Man, a twin to the first,
has been discovered not far from the first dig site.
Then we mentioned that the new artifact would be
kept in the tent with the other artifacts, waiting for
Verona to return and catalogue it. The three of us
are going to keep turns guarding the new "statue,"*

*hoping the thief will come looking for it. Anna has
the first watch, then myself, then Tomas.*

The next sentences were written in different ink,
with a different pen. The new ink matched the number
12 in the date.

*The events of the past several days have been
so disturbing that I have not been able to write
of them until now. Verona was found. And
then lost.*

Lost again? That's some curse. And what was Dad's
burglar trap?

I heard a familiar scream come from outside. Uncle
Stoppard again. I raced out the front door and found
him at the side of the building, tangled in a lilac bush.
A snapped fishing rod was lying on the grass. Jared
was standing half-in, half-out of the bush.

"What happened?" I yelled.

Jared poked his face out of the lilacs. "Nothing real
serious, Finn. Your uncle just fell off the roof."

The hospital waiting room was cold and white.
White walls, white ceiling, white floors. The hard plastic chairs were the color of the guacamole at Cafe Olé.
Jared and I had been sitting in those chairs for about
two hours when a white door at the far end of the
room banged open and we saw a nurse pushing Uncle
Stoppard toward us in a wheelchair.

"It's not broken," said Uncle Stoppard. "Just a
bad sprain."

An aluminum crutch lay across Uncle Stoppard's

lap. In his hand he held a large, white envelope. The temporary cast on his ankle was blue.

"Looks like you're wearing a big blue shoe," said Jared. "Just like in *Cold Feet.*"

Uncle Stoppard groaned.

"Does it hurt bad?" I asked.

"Which one?" said Uncle Stoppard. "The doctor says I should stay off both feet for a week. The puncture needs time to heal, too."

Uncle Stoppard hadn't fallen off the roof, just off the side of the building. While the doctor was examining him, Jared told me what had happened. Back at Cafe Olé, when he and Uncle Stoppard had been talking about fishing, Uncle Stoppard got a couple of ideas for his next mystery novel. All day he must have been boiling over about Mona Trafalgar-Squeer and her pygmy detective. "Let Mona have all the pygmies she wants," Uncle Stoppard had said to Jared. He was going to write about a midget instead. An evil midget. Uncle Stoppard was imagining a book where the villain, not the hero, was a little person. In his book, the midget was a master jewel thief, but Uncle Stoppard couldn't figure out how the midget broke into buildings without being discovered. That's where his second idea—the fishing pole—came in. Uncle Stoppard figured that the midget was also a master angler (that's one of his writer-words for fisherman). The midget would cast a fishing line to the top of a building where the hook would catch and get stuck. Inch by inch, the midget slowly wound the fishing reel, which worked as a kind of pulley system, and hauled himself up the side of the building.

Uncle Stoppard likes to put things in his books that

are true to life. Realistic. Like fingerprints. He needed a real reel for experimenting, so he asked to borrow Jared's. While I had been in my room reading about list-making in Dad's journal, Uncle Stoppard had gone up to the roof of the building and secured the hook after Jared had cast the line up to him. Then Uncle Stoppard went back outside, held on to the fishing rod and began slowly winding in the reel. Jared said that for a few minutes Uncle Stop's idea worked. The reel-pulley really pulled.

"Your uncle was about twelve feet up the side of the building. That fishing line should hold at least two hundred pounds."

"So what happened?" I asked.

"The rod snapped in two," said Jared. "Your uncle landed in a lilac bush."

It was a good thing Uncle Stoppard was wearing his hiking boots. They helped keep the swelling down in his ankle until we reached the hospital.

"Guess what he said when I pulled him out of the lilacs," said Jared.

"What?"

"He looked at me and said, 'I'm bushed.' "

That was Uncle Stoppard all right.

Jared said, "I told him, it looked as though he landed himself a flounder."

I had sure hated leaving the apartment when Jared drove us to the hospital in his black pickup. I was worried something else would be stolen by the time we returned.

When we drove back, Jared and I guided Uncle Stoppard up the apartment stairs and onto the living room couch. It was early evening. I opened up some windows, letting in the delicious cool air. Crickets chatted on the dark lawn.

"Want some ice cream?" Uncle Stoppard asked.

"Thanks," said Jared. "But I should be going. I was supposed to do some laundry on my day off."

"I'll pay for the broken rod," said Uncle Stoppard.

"We'll talk about it later. Take it easy. Bye, dude."

"Bye, Jared," I said.

Uncle Stoppard lay back down on the couch with a sigh. "That, Finnegan, was the stupidest thing your uncle has ever done in his life. Buffoonish."

"It's not that dumb," I said. "I like the idea of a midget climbing up the sides of buildings."

"I even had a title. *A Reel Clever Thief*. Oh, oh. I wonder if that fishing rod is still out there in the grass."

"Don't worry. I'll go pick it up."

Both halves of the fishing rod were still lying in the cool grass. As I picked them up, I noticed that Ms. Pryce had lights on in her apartment. Since her apartment was partly below ground, it was easy to peek in her windows and watch her without being seen. She was wearing one of her all-black outfits, walking through her rooms one by one, lighting red and yellow candles. I knew she was a witch.

As I walked through the front hallway I glanced at the mailboxes. J. Bellini and A. Brazil. So that's who was who. Why did all the women in our building use their first initials? Just like V. Pryce.

By the time I got back to the apartment, Uncle Stoppard was asleep on the couch. All that medicine must have knocked him out. I set the rod and reel quietly on the coffee table, next to his white envelope, and tiptoed back to my bedroom. My dad's journal still lay on the bed. I had forgotten all about Aunt Verona!

April 10

    The events of the past several days have been so disturbing that I have not been able to write of them until now. Verona was found. And then lost.

    Two days ago, Tomas rushed into Anna's and my tent while we were still sleeping. "It's your sister," he cried. Anna and I jumped up from our cots. In the early morning dark, Tomas led us to the locked artifact trailer.

    We couldn't believe our eyes.

    Verona was cautiously exiting the trailer, an empty knapsack over her shoulder and an angry expression in her eyes.

    "Verona," cried Anna. My sister froze. She stared at us. A million thoughts went through my brain. Then she swiftly disappeared behind the trailer. The three of us ran after her. We lost sight of her among the thick shrubbery surrounding the campsite. Then I heard Tomas yelling near the river. Anna and I both reached the riverbank at the same time. "There she is," Tomas said, pointing out over the water. Verona was in a canoe. She must have kept it hidden somewhere to make a fast escape.

    I still couldn't believe that my own sister had stolen artifacts from our dig. Maybe she was planning to take them back to a museum herself and get all the glory. She certainly was one for hog-ging attention.

While we stood there, Tomas reminded us that the river ended in a waterfall not far downstream. We ran back to the Jeep and drove toward the top of the falls. Anna prayed aloud while we sped over the bumpy dirt roads. Tomas even said a few Hail Marys along the way. We reached the falls just in time to see Verona's canoe lurch over the edge. The tiny figure was paddling desperately, but the current was too great. Above the monstrous roar of the falls we heard a horrible scream. It is a sound I will remember as long as I live. Anna turned her head. I watched helplessly as the canoe dropped from sight.

The waterfall is roughly fifty feet in height.

Everyone in our family seems to get into accidents.

The next day, around midnight, the local police pulled a broken and mangled body from the river downstream. I had to go and identify it as my sister. Poor Anna was too distraught.

Pablo and Tomas returned to the campsite where I had found the remains of an old fire on the other side of the river. They dug several holes in the area and found all of the missing gold arti-facts, the crocodile, the plates, the Horizontal Man, and the spoons. I can't believe that all this time Verona was hiding just across the river from us— less than a hundred yards away.

We are making arrangements for Verona's body to be shipped back to the States for burial.

"Finn!" I heard Uncle Stoppard calling me. I ran into the living room.

"What's wrong?" I asked.

"I didn't hear you come back," he said. "I thought something might have happened."

"You were asleep. I didn't want to wake you."

He smiled, but the smile seemed to hurt him. "Would you mind getting me something to drink? Spring water is fine."

When I walked back with Uncle Stoppard's bottle of water from the fridge, he was opening the white envelope he had brought with him from the hospital. "Want the inside scoop on your uncle?" he asked. He pulled out a square sheet of plastic with black splotches on it.

"What's that?" I said.

"My foot. It's an X ray."

I had seen hundreds of X rays on TV before, but never a real one. And never this close. Uncle Stoppard's foot was a gray outline, the bones were an eerie white.

"See?" he said. "No break."

"Lucky break about that lilac bush," I said.

He nodded and took a swig of his water. "What do you think about this for the next book?" he said.

"An X ray of your foot?"

"An X ray of my head. For the inside back cover. Wouldn't that be a cool shot? I could work X rays into the story somehow. Throw me that copy of *Cold Feet*."

He looked at the back of his book and then at the X ray. "Yeah, very cool. And unique," he said. "It would definitely get people's attention. Not just another regular old author headshot."

I liked the idea. "Maybe you could call the new book *Inside Job*," I said.

"Great idea."

"Or *X Marks the Spot.*"

Uncle Stoppard got a funny look on his face. He stared at his book. Then he stared at the X ray. Then he stared at the book again. His cucumber-green eyes grew squinty.

"Definitely brand new," he said. "Hey, Finn, bring me the phone."

I handed him the cordless from the bookshelf near our front door.

"Who are you calling now?" I asked. "It's late."

Uncle Stoppard punched in some numbers, then looked at me. "I think I could use some lemonade."

9
Setting the Trap

The next morning Dad and I hatched a plan to catch the burglar. Dad wasn't there, of course. But his journal was. Uncle Stoppard and I were walking through the cool apartment, eating toast, when Jared knocked at the door. Uncle Stoppard said he had something private to discuss with Jared so I went to my bedroom. I watched the gray raindrops dribble down my window. The only bright spot in the whole room, the photo from Agualar, was now a black hole. Why would someone steal a picture of something they already had? The thief got all the gold he wanted: the Horizontal Man, the spoon, the—wait! The thief did not have the golden spoon. The police had it. But the thief did not know that. The thief might come back looking for that extra piece of Maya treasure. If he— or she—wanted my picture so badly, they must surely want the spoon as well.

That's when I remembered Dad's plan for catching the thief back in Agualar.

I ran back into the living room. Jared and Uncle Stop stopped talking.

"I know how to get proof about Ms. Pryce," I said.

"What are you talking about?" asked Uncle Stoppard.

"Jared said I need proof that Ms. Pryce is the burglar, remember?"

"I thought you said Pablo was the burglar."

"Ms. Pryce is the more likely suspect."

"What's your idea?" asked Uncle Stoppard.

"Simple. We'll set a trap for her."

"A trap?" said Jared.

"It'll be easy," I said. "But first, I have to make a few arrangements." I ran out of the living room, turned around, and ran back in.

"Yes?" said Uncle Stoppard.

"Did you know that Aunt Verona fell over a waterfall down in Agualar?"

Uncle Stoppard looked over at Jared, then back at me. "How did you know that?"

"Dad's journal," I said. "She stole the Horizontal Man and then crashed over the falls."

"The Zwake Curse," said Uncle Stoppard.

Jared shifted on the couch. "Curse?"

"It's complicated," said Uncle Stoppard. "Finn, I, well, I guess I thought it might be too grisly to mention."

Too grisly? After I saw a guy's body turned into mousemeat in the basement? Well, I had plans to make. "See you later," I said.

There were two important things I learned from reading my dad's journal. First, that someone you know, someone close to you, can do things you don't expect. Like Aunt Verona stealing the gold artifacts from the Agualar dig.

Second, I learned that when bad things happen to people, it might be fake. For instance, Pablo got stabbed in the back. But, did he? Ms. Pryce saw a woman flee the building. Did she? Alison's bike was stolen. Was it? Mr. Barrymore threw up in his kilt. Did he? Well, I guess he did—I saw that happen. And smelled it. And Uncle Stoppard did fall off the side of the building. (I didn't actually see him fall, but I saw the broken fishing rod and his motionless body snared in the lilac bush.) But sometimes people can fake you out, especially people you live with, who you see every day. Like Aunt Verona faking out my parents with an overturned canoe. People like her can trick you because you don't expect them to trick you. You trust them.

Now it was my turn to be tricky.

In order for Dad's and my trap to work, everyone in the building had to know about the golden spoon. I was convinced Ms. Pryce had taken it, but what if she had an accomplice? What if her accomplice was Pablo? It was his coffee table that the Horizontal Man had been sitting on. Pablo could have wounded himself with that ski pole and made us all believe he was an innocent victim, just as Aunt Verona had tricked Mom and Dad into thinking she had drowned.

Or perhaps Mr. Barrymore was Ms. Pryce's assistant. Why had he been snooping in the basement? Getting ready for another break-in? When he said "She's lying," was he referring to Ms. Pryce's story about the mysterious running woman? Was he trying to get Ms. Pryce into trouble on purpose? By making us suspect his landlady, Mr. Barrymore would be less of a suspect himself. On the other hand, he might have been talking about Miss Brazil or Miss Bellini. What had they been doing in the basement the night I biked through the neighborhood? I heard them use the word "stealing" when they walked past my kitchen door later that evening. Maybe they had discovered Alison's bike was missing, or maybe they were planning on stealing something themselves. For a nanosecond I was almost glad that the Horizontal Man had been stolen. Until the theft, I never realized what a bunch of creeps lived in our building. Potential creeps is what I mean. Everyone in the building was a potential crook. Or killer. And my trap would not work unless I told everyone about the Maya treasure spoon.

I knocked first at the nurses' apartment. Joan, in a bright yellow sweatsuit this time, answered the door.

"What is it, Finn?"

"Um, I'm missing something and I wondered if you might have seen it."

"Your photo, you mean?" she asked.

"Oh, no, not that. It's my spoon."

Joan looked puzzled. "You want to borrow one of ours?" she asked.

"It's a golden spoon," I said.

"Golden?"

"It belonged to my parents. You know, the archeologists."

"My goodness, real gold?" said Joan. "Where did you last see it?"

"I think it was in my kitchen."

"Do you think the burglar might have stolen that too?"

"I don't know," I said. "But if you see it, will you let me know?"

"Of course," she said. "And I'll let Alison know, too."

"Thanks a lot," I said. "It's from Agualar."

As she shut the door, Joan repeated, "A golden spoon from Agualar. Got it."

I knocked on Mr. Barrymore's door next. When he answered, opening the door only a crack, I repeated my story. Why did I get the feeling he didn't want me to see inside his apartment? Then I went downstairs and fed the same bait to Ms. Pryce.

"More gold?" she said. "You're asking for trouble."

"You think I should call the police?" I asked.

She gave me a mean, hard look. "No. No more police. That's all I need, more shoes tramping in and out of my nice, clean building. More reporters ruining the front lawn." She slammed the door shut.

I was going to pass by Pablo's apartment since he was in the hospital when I heard music from inside. Mariachi music? Someone was listening to the radio or a CD. I knocked on the door, and after about a minute it opened slowly.

"You're back from the hospital," I said.

Pablo looked tired. "Just last night. You want something, Finn?" He was holding a watering can in his hand.

I told him my phony spoon story.

"That same spoon that was in my dish drainer?" he asked. "Now you can't find it?"

"No, and I thought—"

"You thought I took it, huh?"

"Oh, no—"

"Well, if that isn't a kick in the butt," he said.

"Uncle Stoppard says when you get kicked in the butt at least you're moving forward."

Pablo's jaw dropped open. "I'm gonna have to

speak with your uncle tomorrow." He shut the door. " 'Night," he said from inside his apartment.

Well, at least everyone knows, I thought. Step One in my trap was all set. Now I just had to wait until tomorrow before I went ahead with Step Two.

Back in our apartment, Jared was just leaving. Uncle Stoppard said "Thanks," closing the door behind our new friend, the fingerprint cop.

"Did you get the Lemon aid you needed?" I asked.

"I hope so," he said. "But it's only a theory. Where have you been?"

"Working on my trap," I said.

"The one for Ms. Pryce?"

"The trap for whoever is the burglar," I said. "I think it's Ms. Pryce—maybe Pablo—but this way we'll be sure."

"You're not doing something dangerous again, are you?"

"Of course not."

He rubbed his aquiline nose. "So when do I get to hear all about this clever idea of yours?" he asked.

I sat down next to him on the sofa. Since Uncle Stoppard was acting so mysterious about what he and Jared were planning, I decided I could be mysterious, too. "Tomorrow," I said. "That's when we get the Horizontal Man."

Breakfast has become Uncle Stoppard's least favorite meal. I should know better than to try telling him important stuff too early in the day. For example, next morning, while eating my waffles, I quietly and politely explained Step Two of my plan to Uncle Stoppard. His grip tightened on the syrup bottle he was holding, and brown goo squirted all over his lap.

"This is your plan?" he squeaked. "You told me it wasn't dangerous."

"It isn't really."

He wiped syrup from his biker shorts with a wad of paper towels.

"You intend to trap the burglar this evening by spreading the word that there's more treasure?" he said.

"And it's in our apartment," I added.

"You call that not dangerous?" He swabbed some syrup from his navel. "You want me—I mean, us—to end up like Pablo? Or his friend Larry?"

"But we won't be in the apartment when he comes."

"I see. And where will we be?"

"Outside in the lilac bushes," I said.

"But, Finn—"

The trap was very logical. I had already told each resident of our building that I was missing the golden Maya spoon. Next, I had to go back to each person, and say, "Thanks. But I found it. I guess the spoon was in the kitchen all the time." That way everyone will know there is at least one more piece of Agualaran treasure in the apartment. If the thief is as greedy as I think he is, he's got to come looking for it. And if Uncle Stoppard and I pretend to leave the building, and hide outside in the bushes, the thief will come tonight.

"What makes you think he or she will come to-night?" asked Uncle Stoppard.

"Don't you get the feeling that we're being watched?" I said.

He shuddered. "Actually, yes, but—"

"The thief came and stole my photo and my coin the night we were both out of the apartment—and after the police had left. He got into our storage room and took the Horizontal Man without us ever hearing him."

"So?"

"So, he must keep a pretty close watch on us," I said. "He knows when we're gone."

Uncle Stoppard mopped up the last of the syrup that had dribbled onto the floor next to his chair. The dark brown spots on the kitchen tiles reminded me of the dark stains in the storage room downstairs. "But whoever has been stealing things," he said, "is dangerous. They've already killed one person and tried to kill another."

"That's why we'll be outside," I said. "We'll be watching to see who goes into the apartment. I'll watch the front door and you'll watch the back door. Whoever it is wouldn't dare attack us outside in the open with people driving by."

"I'm not so sure."

"We could always call Jared to come over and help."

"Jared would probably try to talk us out of it," said Uncle Stoppard. "Which is what I should do, if I had half a brain. But calling him up is a good idea."

The rest of the day was spent going through more fan mail. And more blue footwear. I counted twenty-six pairs, including some really cool baby-blue motorcycle boots. It was rainy out, so I didn't mind staying inside. And Uncle Stoppard wasn't able to go biking or blading until his two feet healed. That afternoon, I put Step Two into action.

I started with the nurses again. This time A. Brazil answered the door.

"Yeah?"

"I just wanted to let you know I found the spoon," I said.

"Spoon?" asked Alison.

"You know, my golden spoon? The one I was missing."

"Sorry."

"Didn't Joan tell you?"

"She must have forgot. I have to go into work now."

"Just tell her I found it. It was in my kitchen the whole time. The spoon was. The golden spoon from Agualar, okay?"

"Okay."

"Tell her thanks for helping me find my golden spoon."

"I'll tell her."

"From Mexico."

She shut the door.

Mr. Barrymore was not home when I knocked. The plan would only work if everyone knew the same thing. I ran downstairs, grabbed a pen and pad of paper, and wrote a note for Mr. Barrymore. Then I slipped it under his door. I wrote a note for Pablo, too. I figured he was probably resting from his attack.

Ms. Pryce wasn't at home either. When I walked back to our apartment, I heard a swishing sound outside. I found our landlady sweeping branches and leaves from the front walk. The rain must have thrown them down during the night.

"Ms. Pryce," I said. "I found the spoon."

"Good for you." She kept on sweeping and didn't even turn around to face me.

"You know, the golden spoon?" I stared at her black back. She was wearing black jeans, black Army boots, and a black sleeveless sweater. Her sky-blue hair had a black bow in it.

"That's terrific," she said.

"I guess it was in my kitchen the whole time. The golden spoon was."

"Lucky you. Guess you could sell that for a lot of money, huh?"

"Sell it?"

"And move into your own house."

"Oh, I wouldn't sell it," I said. "Uncle Stoppard and I might give it away to a museum, though."

Ms. Pryce finally turned around and looked at me. "Too bad," she said. Then she returned to her sweeping. The broom swishing across the sidewalk sounded like a cat scratching at a door.

"Just thought I'd let you know," I said.

Ms. Pryce did not say another word.

"Well, we're going out tonight. Probably see a movie."

Silence. I returned to our apartment. Uncle Stoppard was working on his computer in his room. I told him that the trap was now all set.

"I couldn't get in touch with Jared," he said. "But I left a message. So what time are we supposed to leave the apartment?"

"As soon as it gets dark," I said.

He glanced at his clock. "That should be around nine o'clock. About five more hours."

"I guess I'll watch TV," I said.

I watched TV, but I didn't see anything. The private screen in my brain was crowded with the faces of our neighbors and the unsmiling, golden face of the Horizontal Man. I was convinced that someone living in our building possessed the statue. Tonight, however, it would be back with its rightful owner, me. Then Uncle Stoppard and I would decide if we should contact the Ackerberg Institute.

Uncle Stoppard hopped out of his room on his crutch at ten minutes after nine. "Still haven't heard from Jared," he said.

I had just finished dressing for our mission. Dark shorts, a gray Minnesota Vikings sweatshirt, sneakers. "Let's go," I said.

"I think we better wait for Jared."

"Just five minutes. It's safe outside."

"It's wet outside."

"It's not raining now," I said.

"In my weakened condition, I should probably wear another sweater. Maybe I should change into long underwear."

"It's not that cold."

"It's damp."

"Wear your jacket," I said, throwing him a wind-breaker from the front closet.

Uncle Stoppard grumbled something about "pneumonia" while he hobbled out the back door. But I knew he was excited about trapping the burglar. How could he not be? This real-life experience would probably end up in one of his books. I locked the front door, turned out all the lights, and met Uncle Stoppard outside by the waterspout.

"I'll go around and watch the front door," I whispered.

"Where should I stand?" Uncle Stoppard asked.

"There are lilac bushes all over the place. That big one, by the garage."

Uncle Stoppard hopped over to the bush. "I should have brought a hankie." He stopped hopping and turned to look at me. "What about protection?"

"Protection?"

"For self-defense," he said. "I'll go back inside and get one of those ski poles."

"Look," I said. "There's a car going through the alley. Cars drive by all the time. This will be safe."

"Five minutes, then we're going in."

"Five minutes, then we'll meet back here. It might take longer for the burglar to break in."

"It feels like rain," said Uncle Stoppard.

"I'm going around front," I said. "If I see Jared, I'll come back and let you know."

Uncle Stoppard gave me the thumbs-up sign and then sneezed into his hand. He shouldn't have worn his glasses; the lenses reflected lights from the building next door. That's why I left my own glasses inside on my dresser. In order for my trap to work, we both needed to be totally hidden in the dark bushes. As if the neighbors could read my mind, the lights from next door blinked out. Ah, good. Uncle Stoppard was now completely invisible.

I crept quietly over the darkened lawn toward the front of the building. The largest lilac bush was at the corner. I squeezed behind it, the glossy wet leaves smearing rain all over my sweatshirt and shorts. The lights were turned off in Ms. Pryce's apartment. Candles flickered inside on a small glass table in her front room. Doing her witch stuff again, I figured. Where was she?

Though I had a good view of the front sidewalk, and of our landlady's apartment, I couldn't see the door to our apartment inside the front hall. Maybe I should run across the street and hide in a bush over there. I would have a perfect straight-shot view of our door.

Or I could hide in the street, ducked behind one of the parked cars.

I heard a knock at Ms. Pryce's front door. A shadow moved inside the apartment, her door opened, the light from the hallway fell on her face and hair.

Her visitor was Mr. Barrymore. He seemed very excited. I couldn't hear any words through the closed window, except what sounded like "Brazil." Then Ms. Pryce got excited. Or upset. I couldn't tell which. She said something like "I'll kill her" or "I'll kill him." Then Mr. Barrymore left with a weird smile on his face. Five minutes later, after pacing furiously back and forth, mumbling to herself, Ms. Pryce left, too. The candlelight made spooky silhouettes on the lonely walls of her apartment.

I wanted to see where Ms. Pryce and Mr. Barrymore had gone. I took a step backward and collided with a body. A tall body. A heavy hand fell on my shoulder. With a gasp, I spun around and stared. Mr. Barrymore was staring back, breathing hard, a finger to his lips.

"Don't say a word," said Mr. Barrymore.

His face, with the furry caterpillar eyebrows, was shadowed by thick lilac leaves. A light fell on both of us. Mr. Barrymore took a step back. I could see him glancing behind me, through the windows of Ms. Pryce's apartment.

"Not a single word," he whispered.

I turned and saw that Ms. Pryce had reentered her front room and switched on a lamp. Joan and Alison were right behind her. Joan was wearing a bright purple sweatsuit. She looked like a big grape. Alison looked angry. She stood with her fists on her hips, while Ms. Pryce waved her hands around.

"What's going on?" I said.

I turned back to look at Mr. Barrymore, but he grabbed my shoulder. "Don't make any sudden moves," he said. "Oh, no—"

He covered his face with his hands.

I heard noises. Ms. Pryce was staring at the window. Staring at me. She yelled something I couldn't understand. Then all three women ran out of the apartment.

I stood for a second, deciding whether to follow the women, tell Uncle Stoppard about Mr. Barrymore's odd behavior, or remain hidden behind the lilacs and keep watching for the burglar to make his move. My trap was not working. This was not supposed to happen.

I heard Alison shouting at the back door of the apartment building. Mr. Barrymore groaned. I ran back to see what was going on and found the two nurses anxiously searching the backyard.

"There you are!" said Alison, turning on me. "Where is he?"

"Yes, where did he go?" Joan said.

"Who are you talking about?"

"Barrymore!" said Alison.

"He's spreading rumors about Alison," said Joan. "He said she stole her own bike and then blamed it—"

"That's enough," said Alison. Then she turned back to me, her eyes red and puffy. "Have you seen that Barrymore creature?"

"Well—"

"You have!" said Alison.

"Where is he, Finn?" asked Joan. "We simply want to talk with him."

"I simply want to murder him," said Alison.

"Well, um, the last time I saw him—"

"Yes?"

"I, uh, think I saw him walking up to his apartment."

Both nurses disappeared inside the back door. I decided to follow them. I was sorry I lied to them about Mr. Barrymore's location, but I didn't want them running around outside and making lots of noise, scaring away any potential burglars.

"His door's open," Alison yelled at the top of the flight of stairs.

I saw Joan disappear into Mr. Barrymore's apartment. I was running right behind her. A loud thud and the crash of breaking glass filled the back hallway.

"Look out!" hollered Joan.

It's a good thing I wasn't wearing my glasses. As soon as I entered Mr. Barrymore's apartment, I slipped on a puddle of water and slid feet first into Joan's head. Joan was horizontal on the floor. She had collided with Alison. All of us were on our backs, surrounded by broken glass, water, and dozens of flopping goldfish.

"Careful," said Joan. "There's glass everywhere."

"What is this?" cried Alison.

Mr. Barrymore's apartment was a giant aquarium. More than a hundred fishbowls covered his tables, bookshelves, radiators, rugs, chairs. Each fishbowl contained a single, shimmery goldfish. A small green label was fixed to each of the bowls. I cautiously stood up, my shorts and sweatshirt dripping onto the polished hardwood floor. Taking a closer look at one of the labeled bowls, I read: "Property of Animal Preserve, Inc. Name: Goldie 23." *Animal Preserve?* Where had I heard that name before?

Joan and Alison had also gotten to their feet.

Ms. Pryce appeared in Mr. Barrymore's dining room. "What is this mess?" she screamed. "No pets! I tell everyone, no pets!" Blue electrical sparks practically fizzed off her head.

"How many fish does one guy need?" said Joan.

"He's twisted," said Alison. "And we still need to find him."

Ms. Pryce pointed a witchy finger at me. "What on earth are you doing?"

I figured it looked pretty clear what I was doing. Scooping up flopping, bug-eyed goldfish from among the shattered glass on the floor, and throwing them into nearby bowls. Four in one bowl, five in another. Mr. Barrymore would have to sort them all out later. How can you tell goldfish apart?

"I thought you were going to a movie," Ms. Pryce said. She put her hands on her hips and turned to the nurses. "I saw this kid with Barrymore. He was out by the lilac bush."

Joan and Alison stared at me. They raced past Ms. Pryce and out the apartment door, their shoes squishing loudly all the way down the stairs.

"Wait 'til I catch that joker," said Ms. Pryce.

I rushed out the apartment, hip-hopping over the puddles and glass, and beat Ms. Pryce to the bottom of the back stairs. The two nurses were standing by the garage.

"There he is," said Joan, pointing to the big bush in the backyard.

"No," I said, "that isn't him. That's—"

The nurses had seen a figure skulking among the lilac leaves and decided it was their evil third-floor, kilt-wearing, fish-loving neighbor. Alison flew through the air like an All-American nose-tackle. I heard Joan yell, "Get him!" I heard Uncle Stoppard shout, "Uncle!" Lilac leaves rustled furiously as if whipped by a tornado. Then, silence.

Joan and Alison pulled a wilted figure from the dark bush.

"I am so sorry," said Joan.

"We thought you were Barrymore," said Alison. "Pryce said that—"

"Finn," said Uncle Stoppard. There was blood dripping from his lip. "Can you get my crutch, please."

"Crutch?" asked Alison.

"We beat up a guy on crutches?" gasped Joan.

Uncle Stoppard smiled weakly. "Only one crutch."

"And we're registered nurses!" Joan said to her roommate.

"I'm just glad you're not Sumo wrestlers," said Uncle Stoppard.

I fetched the crutch, which had been trampled into the soft mud during the attack, while the two health professionals ushered Uncle Stoppard back to his familiar resting place on the couch in the living room.

"What happened to your foot?" said Alison. "I mean, the other one."

"A fishing accident," said Uncle Stoppard. "Why are your clothes all wet?"

"A fishing accident," said Joan.

"Why were you hiding out there?" asked Alison. "You looking for Barrymore, too?"

"Don't tell me he's the burglar."

Alison sighed. "No, he's just a Grade-A jerk."

Uncle Stoppard rubbed his eyes. "Finn, I must have, uh, dropped my glasses outside. Could you run and get those for me, too?"

As I ran down the hallway to our kitchen door, I could hear Joan moaning behind me in the living room, "A man on crutches wearing glasses!"

It was not as easy finding Uncle Stoppard's glasses as it was his crutch. For one thing, glasses are smaller. After searching carefully for ten minutes, I found them snagged on a skinny branch, dangling a foot above the wet grass. At least they didn't get dirty. And it looked as if both lenses were unbroken.

I folded the glasses into the pocket of my sweatshirt. As I stepped out from the lilac bush, a pair of strong arms grabbed me from behind. A dark sack like a pillowcase was pulled over my head. The strange arms held me down against a big, powerful knee, and my hands were tied behind my back.

10
Trunk

I heard the lid of a car trunk bang shut over my head. I heard the lock click. I heard the roar of the engine and the crackle of gravel sprayed by the car's tires. As the car sped forward, I was thrown to the back of the trunk. With my hands tied behind me, I couldn't take off the dark bag that was over my head. Everything had happened so fast, that by the time I thought of yelling for Uncle Stoppard it was too late.

But before I heard the engine roar I heard the thunk-thunk of two car doors closing. Two. The burglar did have an accomplice. When the powerful hands were holding me down across that big knee, it was another pair of hands that did the tying. Ms. Pryce and Mr. Barrymore. They were working together. Where were they taking me?

It was the Zwake Curse. First Aunt Verona, then Mom and Dad, then Uncle Stoppard with his feet (even though he wasn't a Zwake, but a Sterling—actually a Bumpelmeyer), and now me. I was being kidnapped at the speed of sixty miles an hour.

The car, probably Ms. Pryce's brand-new one, kept turning corners and throwing me back and forth inside the dark, smelly trunk. I couldn't tell which direction they were taking me. Why would they take me some-place else? Why didn't they just steal the spoon, or else keep me locked up in Ms. Pryce's apartment? Or Mr. Barrymore's place?

Ransom! They were going to call Uncle Stoppard and exchange me for the golden spoon of Agualar. That was it. Ms. Pryce and Mr. Barrymore must have realized I was setting a trap for them. Somehow they saw through my clever story of the spoon's disappear-ance and reappearance. They figured it would be eas-ier to kidnap me and ask for the spoon instead of searching the kitchen for it.

I had always heard stories on TV about people being kidnapped. This was what it felt like.

I would never see Uncle Stoppard again.

I would never see my parents again.

I would never go to school again.

We would never move to a house with a yard big enough for a dog.

My hands were tied too tight. The rope was too skinny for me to try and grab with my groping fingers. I thought of kicking against the trunk, but no one would hear me on the street or highway. And it might make my kidnappers mad. If they heard me, they might stop the car and do something worse.

What if I kicked in the other direction? I could move the backseat. I know there would be no escape in that direction, but I might overhear what the kid-nappers planned to do with me. They might give me a clue about where we were headed.

I pushed against the backseat, but not too hard. Slowly, it inched forward. I heard a radio playing rock music. I could also hear the kidnappers talking—not clearly—but I could tell there were two of them. A man and a woman. The woman did most of the talking. She did not sound like Ms. Pryce. In fact, a few times she sounded as if she were speaking another language. Was it—?

Spanish! That's what the language was.

It wasn't Mr. Barrymore in the car with Ms. Pryce. It was Pablo. I was right all along. That's why the Horizontal Man was sitting on his coffee table. Because Pablo had stolen it. And when Ms. Pryce saw that I noticed the statue that day, when I dropped off Pablo's package, she must have snatched it up when I went back to my apartment.

That means Pablo had faked his attack. Ms. Pryce must have hit him according to their plan, but she didn't know her own strength, so Pablo ended up in the hospital with a punctured lung.

To throw the police off her track, Ms. Pryce lied about seeing that strange woman running out of our building.

But why would Pablo kill his friend Larry? Did Ms. Pryce kill him by accident? Was Larry actually another accomplice, who got greedy and started stealing behind Pablo's back? Maybe Larry found out about Pablo and Ms. Pryce's scheme and blackmailed them. But, that still didn't explain why Pablo put a new lock on the room that he was stealing from. Changing padlocks only drew more attention to the storage room, and told us that Pablo had been down there recently. Why not leave the old lock, go on quietly stealing gold from beneath our very noses, and then move back to Agualar, or wherever it was he came from? And why give us a new set of keys? Was he trying to confuse us? Something was wrong.

Yuck! Cigarette smoke. I hate that smell. I had to be careful not to cough, or the kidnappers would know the backseat had been moved. Well, the woman was not Ms. Pryce. She hates cigarettes.

I heard the man kidnapper talking. He was also speaking in a foreign language. But it didn't sound like Pablo's voice.

Who were these people?

Two kidnappers. Spanish. Mariachi music. Cafe Olé.

Hmmm, people in Mexico speak Spanish. And in Agualar. Dad wrote in his journal that some of the Agualarans thought that the ancient Maya gold really belonged to them. Were the kidnappers actual spies sent to recapture their treasure, and two of them had captured me? Were they out for revenge?

A quick swerve of the car caused me to bump my head against the side of the trunk.

We were barreling southward, on our way to Agualar, where I would end up as a sacrificial victim to an ancient Maya cult. Two Zwakes had dug up and disturbed Maya soil, and now one Zwake must pay. I would be chained to a stone slab, hot sunlight burning in my eyes, a gold, feathered dagger held inches over my heart by an unsmiling priest speaking a foreign language.

The car jolted again. I thought back to the lists I made in Dad's journal. My list of suspects included everyone in the apartment building, but these people in the car were strangers. At least, they *sounded* like strangers. If it was someone from my list, why would they disguise their voices in the car? Or more likely, the voices they used in real life, the voices they used in the apartment building when they spoke to their neighbors every day, were the phony voices. They were putting on an act.

Actors? Strangers?

The car stopped so suddenly, I banged my head against the back of the seat. Could they tell the seat had moved? I heard two car doors open and shut. I also heard other cars and trucks whizzing and rumbling by. Fast. We must have been near a freeway.

I heard the loud squeal of a truck's air brakes. Then I heard a familiar *ding-ding*—the sound cars make when they run over those hoses at the gas stations. We were at a gas station or a truck stop.

I wonder how far we had traveled? I had lost track of time in the darkness of the trunk. We might be miles south of Minneapolis. The gas station might be in Iowa or Nebraska or Kansas.

I didn't want to go to Mexico. I'm from Minnesota, I hate hot weather.

I want to go to nice, cool, refreshing Iceland.

I'm so glad that Dad and Mom decided not to take me with them on their expedition to Tquuli. I'm so glad they left me behind with stupid Uncle Stoppard so he could protect me and keep me out of danger.

What was going on? Where had the two strangers gone? It seemed I was waiting for hours for them to open the trunk. Were they going to abandon me in this car, leaving me to starve?

Right now, I'd even eat a slice of raisin toast.

Should I kick against the back of the trunk? Yell for help? Some Iowan or Nebraskan walking by might hear me. The kidnappers might hear me, too. What if they were standing just outside the car? I did not want to make them angry.

Voices. Then the *thunk-thunk* of the two car doors opening and closing again. The engine roared and we were off again.

The darkness seemed to last forever until the car stopped again. I heard no cars or trucks driving by. No *ding-dings*. I heard a crackling sound. Static. The voices were arguing. The woman said something in English, something about the radio not working. He yelled something, then she answered it wasn't her fault. The radio didn't work because of where we were. Where are we? A tunnel? Underground? Inside a warehouse or garage?

A humming sound. Someone was using an automatic window opener. Then I heard a loud pounding. No, it was chirping, the chirping of crickets. Thousands of them. Maybe millions. We were somewhere in the country, next to a field or farm. I must have been sleepy, because I imagined the billion crickets were chirping with a Spanish accent. Insect mariachi music. A cool breeze filtered back through the opening behind the backseat, and brushed the bag against my face.

The voices sounded again. Quiet and low. Followed by a slurping sound. Hmmm, they kissed each other. Good night? I guess they were going to sleep.

I wondered if Uncle Stoppard was sleeping. How could he sleep knowing that I was in the trunk of a strange car? But how would he know that? He might think I was off exploring the neighborhood again, riding my bike, hunting for clues.

He might still be sitting on the couch, blood dripping from his lip, his two wounded feet propped up in front of him, waiting for me and his missing glasses. How much time had gone by since I had been snatched from the lilac bush? How much time did I have left?

Now was the time to plot my escape.

It is not difficult getting out of the locked trunk of a car. It's simply a matter of finding the metal catch at the back of the trunk and pulling it free with your fingers or with a tool like a screwdriver. What makes it difficult is opening a trunk when your hands are tied behind your back and two kidnappers are asleep in the front seat.

Uncle Stoppard says timing is everything. I had to wait until I was sure the kidnappers were sound asleep. I slowly inched backwards toward the catch, making sure to make no sound or movements that would rock the car. I could feel the grimy latch with my fingers. I placed my fingers carefully and then took a deep breath. I couldn't predict whether the latch would open with a bang or a small pop. I was praying for the small pop.

What I wasn't expecting to hear was a scratching sound. Just outside the trunk. Scratching? Paws? A bear was trying to get into the trunk! His razorlike claws mere inches from my head. The bear would wake the kidnappers and I'd never get out of this car.

Silence. No sound of clawing, or puffing, or the padding of heavy, hairy feet came from outside. I lay perfectly still. After waiting for a few million years, I decided to continue with my original plan, bear or no bear. I would rather take my chances with a wild beast than with a pair of devious human spies who smoked cigarettes.

My fingers found the latch again and pulled. The hood released with a medium-sized pop and a metallic sigh. I lay dead still. No sound from within the car. The sleepers slept. Still hooded with the sack, my hands still tied behind me, I quietly pulled my legs toward my butt in the fetal position. With all the speed of a snail, I shifted my head and shoulders over my knees. My head pushed gently upward against the underside of the hood. The hood lifted a few inches. Again I stood still. And still no sound from the two kidnappers.

This was it. I would get no second chance. But wait! What about that scratching sound? I had read stories about bears chasing hunters and campers up trees, and then waiting for hours for the humans to grow hungry and climb back down. Could an extremely patient bear be lurking just outside the trunk? Lying on the ground, a breathing, furry shadow, jaws open wide, waiting for a stupid kid to reach out with his soft, eatable foot? Since I'm right-handed, I decided to step out with my left foot first.

I lifted my leg over the side of the trunk and then froze. My shorts and bare thighs straddled the cold metal for a million years. No sound. No breathing. Not the whisper of a heavy paw groping through the air. Not even the wet crunch of invisible teeth through human ankle bones. I figured it was a good sign and half-hopped, half-pulled my right leg out. Then I ran.

I fell into a bush. At least it didn't have claws or fangs. I couldn't see a thing with the stupid bag on my head, but I had enough sense of direction to know that running around to the other side of the bush would hide me from the kidnappers, at least for a moment, if they heard me. Standing straight up, away from the dark, claustrophobic trunk, gave me a sense of freedom. I sat down on the wet, unseen grass, and wriggled my hands down over my butt, around my legs, and under my ankles.

With my hands now in front of me, I tore the bag off my head. Cool air. A million stars dotted a dark sky above the tall shapes of pine trees. I didn't have time to figure out where I was. I spun around and peered past the bush.

Starlight gleamed on the chrome and windows of the car, parked just off the road in what looked like the middle of a huge forest. The kidnapper's trunk yawned open like some enormous hippopotamus mouth. Or bear mouth. But no evidence of bears any-where. The car did not look like Ms. Pryce's, but I didn't actually get a good look at it the other night in the alley when she almost ran me over. My mind was on other things.

In the dim light, I could see the knots that held my wrists. I yanked at them with my teeth, and in a few minutes I was free. But free to go where? Besides being sweaty, grimy, smelly, wet and hungry, I had absolutely no idea where I was.

I walked in the opposite direction the car was fac-ing. Quickly. Huge pine trees lined both sides of the two-lane asphalt road. A dark, cricket-infested jungle closed in on me, a band of star-dotted sky overhead. The back of my neck prickled; I felt bright, burning eyes staring at me from the bushes. Did those eyes belong to the bear, or whatever creature had tried to claw its way into the car trunk? Or just some wary deer or fox trying to stay out of danger? My legs were stiff, but it felt good to walk. I started to run. Eventually, I hoped, another car would come along. I could hitch a ride to the nearest town and call the police.

A square shadow loomed up next to the road. A sign. I walked to the other side and squinted up at the words painted in white against a dark green background: Impact, 6 miles. Impact? That sounded familiar.

The sign stood at a crossroads. The road I was walking on crossed another two-lane asphalt road at right angles. Now where should I go? There were no lights in any direction. I decided to turn right and keep moving.

I was glad I was wearing my gray Viking sweatshirt with all the pockets because the air felt cold on my bare legs. A lot colder than back in Minneapolis. I thought it was supposed to get warmer the further south you traveled. And the kidnappers must have been driving for hours. We should be in Mexico by now. Or at least Iowa.

Oh, great! Another car was finally driving down the road, coming from the direction of the Impact sign. I turned around and waved at the lights. The car slowed. I could see there was just the driver in the car.

"Need a ride?" he said.

"Yeah, could you take me—"

There was a movement next to him on the front seat. A second passenger. A woman. He pushed her head down so I wouldn't see it. But I had already recognized the man's voice. These were the kidnappers.

I ran off the road and into the pine forest. I heard car doors open, and the man yelling in Spanish. I didn't waste any time looking back.

The stars gave just enough light to see my way around the tall trunks. I ran as fast as I could. Footsteps crunching on pine needles and branches kept following me for what seemed like hours. My path took me into an unexpected clearing, a wide circle of grass surrounded by smaller pine trees. I would be more easily seen out in the open, so I stayed inside the shadow of the taller trees, skirting my way to the left. When I got to the other side of the clearing, I paused to catch my breath. No sounds except for the cricket orchestra and an occasional owl hoot. The kidnappers had stopped. At least, they had stopped running. They might be walking quietly over the forest floor, so I wouldn't hear them until it was too late.

Who was the driver? It had been too dark to see his face.

The forest was growing lighter. Tree trunks were gray and brown now, not black like before. Pine needles rustled above me. It must be early morning. I figured it was late, since the moon wasn't in the sky, but I didn't realize how late. It must be close to four or five. Let's see, that would mean the kidnappers and I had been on the road for about six or seven hours. Six times sixty miles per hour—I was at least three hundred and sixty miles from home!

The growing light meant the kidnappers, or bears, could spot me more easily. I stayed hunched down behind a tree trunk. All around me were more tree trunks and a few small bushes. I didn't see any sign of humans, though I did see a red fox darting between the pines. I looked back through the clearing. Still no sign of kidnappers. I saw something else, something that had been there all the time at the corner of my eye, something I had thought was clouds or hills behind the tall pines. Cliffs of gray, treeless rock. The cliffs stretched as far as I could see, far beyond the clearing. They seemed to curve in a gigantic arc.

Now I knew where I was. The only place in Minnesota, three hundred miles from home, where there were cliffs like these. That's why the name Impact was familiar.

Straddling the Minnesota-Canadian border, not far from Lake Superior, is a monster crater made by a meteor crashing into the Earth millions of years ago. French explorers discovered it in the 1700s and dubbed it La Grand Fosse, which basically means the Big Hole. Old-timers call it the Great Depression. Fifteen miles across and over two hundred feet deep, the bottom bowl of the crater contains a huge forest, a lake, a waterfall, and wild animals found nowhere else on earth. The governments of America and Canada decided to call it Grand Meteor International Forest, and made it a joint two-country park, with the borderline stretching right through the middle of the forest. Near the center of the Big Hole is the small Canadian-American town of Impact.

Everyone who's gone to school in Minnesota has heard all about the Grand Meteor Forest. I'd never been here before, but I always wanted to camp here. Because of the incredible cliffs. And because of the famous—

A huge brown shape shifted behind some trees to my left. Another shape, a small mountain of fur and claws, followed the first. A third. And a fourth.

Since I knew I was in the Grand Meteor Forest, I was no longer afraid of bears. Bears did not live in the Big Hole. Raccoons, however, did. Giant raccoons. Raccoons so enormous that the fur from only two or three creatures could supply a thick winter coat for a grown adult.

The same French explorers who named the crater also named the beasts King raccoons, for King Louie. That's what my teacher had said. A family of four, no five, Louies was slowly trundling toward me. These could be the same creatures who clawed the trunk of the car. What did they want with me? Breakfast? I was beginning to develop a strong dislike for rodents of all sizes.

They were impressive, though. The biggest Louie (the mom or dad) was the size of a motorcycle. A Harley. Its shiny black eyes were 8-balls, its teeth were ivory daggers. The deadly paws, scraping along the leaf-covered ground, were as big as baseball mitts. I had heard about the 8-balls and the daggers and the baseball mitts from a video on Minnesota mammals back in fifth grade. Now I was seeing them for real, eyeball to 8-ball. What had the video said about raccoon eating habits? Fish? Roots? Teenage-boys? Even if I wasn't the raccoons' idea of waffles and orange juice, I didn't want to stick around and find out. If I ever got out of the Big Hole alive, I promised myself to pay more attention during history and science class. And if Uncle Stoppard ever asked me to join him while he watched some boring documentary on TV, I would gladly sit with him through the biggest yawners in the history of television, and memorize every single boring, life-saving word.

The raccoons began to circle me. Like vultures. The hugest King Louie was in the lead, the smaller ones trailing closely behind. Even the smaller creatures' claws reminded me of dangerous garden tools. A single talon could rip open my bare leg. If the raccoons were only curious, and not threatening, they might still accidentally slash me and leave me to bleed to death in the middle of nowhere.

As they scooted across the leafy ground, the creatures hissed and jabbered, their jaws crammed full of sharp, pointy teeth. How could one animal have so many teeth? My stomach growled and one of the creatures stopped to stare directly at me. He looked hungry. Maybe he was sizing me up, trying to decide if I would be enough of a meal for the five of them. Trying to decide which piece of me to grab first when the feasting began. Or maybe he was wondering what flavor I was. When Uncle Stoppard finishes writing a book, he treats himself to a box of expensive chocolates. But you can never tell how one of those chocolates will taste until you actually bite into it. That's what the staring raccoon was thinking. Was I a nougat or a mint? Dark chocolate or milk chocolate? There was only one way to find out. Five black noses sniffed along the ground, leading them slowly, but surely, along a tightening spiral with me at the center. The creamy center!

I shot through the clearing, leaping over the smallest of the raccoons. Quickly gaining the opposite side, I plowed a path past the bushes and trees as quickly as

I could. The Louies grunted. I heard rustling close behind me. Branches whipped me, cutting at my hands and face as I ran. Thick bushes scraped my bare legs, but I felt no pain. I only felt the ground slamming against my sneakers with each step. The only sound was the thumping of my heart and the thud of heavy feet plodding and jostling somewhere behind me.

The bushes ended abruptly. A rushing stream flowed across the woods, directly in my escape path. It didn't look very deep. The first step I took froze my feet. The cold seeped right through my sneakers and into my bones. Taking a deep breath, I plunged forward. After a few seconds, I didn't think about the cold. Instead, I kept thinking of those giant claws slashing their way through the forest.

Halfway across the stream, the water rose to my armpits. I turned to look back at the bank. The five Louies had arrived at the water's edge and were sniffing furiously. The adult Louie stared at me. I turned forward and half-swam, half-waded my way up to the opposite bank. I wasn't sure if raccoons could swim or not. I hoped not. If they did, maybe the water would slow them down while I kept running through the rest of the forest.

"I heard him over here!" The male kidnapper's voice came from behind the raccoon family. The startled Louies scattered into the bushes alongside the stream.

"No, over here." The man stepped out from the forest. I had never seen him before in my life. He was tall and muscular with strong, brown arms and a thick black mustache. He carried a hunting knife in his right hand. He must have used that to slash at the branches in his path.

I had slipped behind a tree at the sound of his voice. He didn't see me. His attention seemed to be caught by something in the bushes. "I found him," yelled the man to his companion. She was nowhere in sight, still hidden among the trees on the other side of the stream. In a lower voice I heard him say, "Here's his sweater." The man grabbed at something. A terrific roar echoed through the forest. One of the raccoons! No, it was actually the kidnapper screaming! The man must have mistaken one of the Louies for my gray sweatshirt and reached for it. The offended Louie pounced from the leafy bushes and snarled at him. The man yelled his lungs out. The frightened raccoon yelled back.

The man raised his knife, but from another bush, a monster adult raccoon leaped out. The man screamed again, and stumbled into the bushes to escape. But he accidentally stumbled into the other three hiding Louies. He must have thought the woods were stuffed full of them. He swung around wildly. The hissing raccoons outflanked him. There was nothing for him to do but plunge into the icy cold stream. The more intelligent animals stayed on shore.

While the kidnapper swore at the raccoon family through chattering teeth, the Louies calmly cleaned their silvery gray fur and stared at the curious intruder. In a few minutes, though, the animals seemed to grow bored and waddled off upstream. I stepped out from my hiding place and continued my escape. I heard the man sloshing through the water, yelling behind me. I also heard more grunts and sniffs. What were the Louies up to now?

Within the shadowy forest, there was no way to see the giant cliffs, and therefore no way to tell which direction I was heading. If I could just see them and keep the cliffs behind me, I knew I would be running toward the center of the crater and would eventually arrive at the town of Impact. Of course, the kidnappers might guess I would look for the town. What if I headed toward the cliffs instead? I remembered where the stream lay. If I followed its path, traveled upstream, I should arrive at higher ground. The cliffs.

My stomach growled as I scrambled over the forest floor. If I kept running, I felt warmer. My sneakers squished, but my socks and shorts were drier now. I heard the snap of a breaking twig behind me, but I never saw a thing. No sign of the tall man with the knife or of the Louies.

The forest grew thinner up ahead. I approached another clearing, larger than the last, but still no sign of the town. No road, no house, no telephone poles. Was I even headed in the right direction? The cliffs were nowhere in sight. As I crossed the clearing, I heard a strange droning. Two helicopters zoomed overhead. It was no use waving and shouting, but I did it anyway. The copters turned into dots in the sky and disappeared.

There must be some way to get their attention, I thought. If they come back. Discouraged, I jammed my fists into the front pocket of my sweatshirt. Uncle Stoppard's glasses! I had forgotten all about them. Luckily I didn't break them while I was thrown around in the kidnappers' trunk.

Something else was in my pocket. Something wet and gross. I pulled out two dead goldfish from my sweatshirt. They must have landed in there when I slipped on the puddle in Mr. Barrymore's apartment. That's what the Louies were after!

I gazed down at the damp, fishy glasses in my hands. I wished Uncle Stoppard was wearing them right now, standing beside me. I thought of how Uncle Stoppard always wished he could wear contacts, but the doctors said his eyeballs were shaped too funny for them to work. He hated wearing the thick lenses. He said he looked geekish. I thought he looked cool.

The plastic frames felt warm in my hands. I gazed up toward the sky. The helicopters were still missing.

But the sun was still there. I had a major idea.

I ran around the clearing gathering dry grass, fallen pine needles, and scrunchy leaves that had fallen or been blown off some of the small bushes scattered around. I heaped them into a small pile. Then I held Uncle Stoppard's glasses between the sunlight and my little heap of kindling.

The sunlight focused into a tiny, white dot. The dot fell on one of the dried-out leaves. A tiny whiff of whitish smoke coiled up from the leaf. It was working. Uncle Stoppard's glasses worked as a magnifying lens. In a few moments, the whole heap would catch fire and send a smoke signal into the air. The helicopters would spot the smoke and circle back. I would be rescued.

"Hey!"

I heard a yell and turned. It was the man with the knife. He was running into the clearing straight toward me. I was still on my knees, still focusing the sunlight onto the fire. The guy would be on top of me in seconds. Then I saw that the man was not alone. Five furry shapes quietly entered the clearing behind him. A weird image flashed through my brain. I wondered if the raccoons would eat my remains after the guy had killed me there in the forest. And that reminded me of Mona Trafalgar-Squeer. Mona wrote a mystery called *Tiny, Bloody Remains*—it was one of her earliest books, and one of her best—about a crazed biologist who works at a petting zoo. Uncle Stoppard didn't like the book; he said it was the product of Mona's "tiny, bloody mind." Mona's killer-biologist uses the animals at the zoo to bump off his victims in various ways: an army of ducklings cause a traffic accident, deer stampede over unsuspecting picnickers, and baby raccoons have their paws painted with poison. I remembered a scene where the baby raccoons were being fed by the killer. Who needs a documentary when I have Mona? But I must admit, I never felt the same way about petting zoos after that book. Anyway, the baby raccoons were fed fish. Fish was their favorite food.

I stood up just as the man approached me. I dug into my pockets and found at least six more of the poor dead creatures from Mr. Barrymore's apartment. As the man lunged at me, I flung the orange carcasses into his face. He brushed them away and swore at me. But the raccoons pounced. Breakfast was served. Five hungry Louies surrounded the man, sniffing out the shiny, wet bodies on his clothes and in the grass. The man screamed again, slapping at his clothing and stomping his feet. I think he must have a thing about mammals.

I shoved Uncle Stoppard's glasses back into my pocket and ran. I was yards ahead of the kidnapper when I stopped to look back. The man had now been joined by the woman. While the raccoons rooted out fallen fish in the grass, and the man kept brushing at his clothes, the woman kicked apart my makeshift fire. She stomped on the leaves. Uncle Stoppard's smoke evaporated in the bright morning air.

She pointed at me and yelled at her companion. "The knife! Use the knife, you idiot!"

I turned, breathless, pain stabbing in my left side. The woman. I had seen her once before. And not back in Minneapolis in the apartment building. I had seen her short, dark hair and shining eyes in an old photograph.

It was Aunt Verona.

11
Face to Face

My aunt never fell over that waterfall in Agualar. She had faked out Mom and Dad once with the empty canoe on the river. She did it again by going over the waterfall. She must have always had an escape plan. Who was the broken and mangled body that the police pulled out of the river the next day? Some poor Hispanic woman who was killed to protect my aunt? Did that mean Aunt Verona was a killer?

It's hard to believe that anyone in my family could kill another human being. Then again, maybe that's who the strange guy was. I mean, maybe the driver of the car was the actual murderer. As Uncle Stoppard might call him, he was the muscles of the team. His arms were certainly big and powerful. I had suggested to Uncle Stoppard that there were two people working together to steal my gold—I mean, the Maya gold—a burglar and a killer. Unfortunately, I was right.

I thought of the female flesh and blood the Agualaran police pulled from the river. The body that Dad identified as Verona Zwake. The face must have been hard to recognize. Like Larry's face after the rats had finished dinner. Dad was probably so upset about seeing Aunt Verona tumble over the waterfall that he couldn't think straight, couldn't see straight. He must have imagined the body resembled his sister. Who would have guessed that Verona had tricked them a second time? That she would even dare?

Aunt Verona was the curse of the Zwake family.

My brain and body were on fire as I raced away from the kidnappers.

I heard her yell a second time. "Use your knife!"

The shock of hearing those words slowed me down. Aunt Verona wouldn't let that guy hurt me, would she? I was her nephew. Her flesh and blood. I turned to look at her. Instead, I saw the man, less than fifty feet away. He pulled the knife from his belt—too bad the raccoons hadn't run off with it—and aimed.

Verona shouted, "Throw it!" Some relative.

The tall man started at me and aimed his knife. He held it high above his head. I didn't even think of ducking out of the way. Aunt Verona's cruel words echoed in my head, turning my feet to stone.

The man yelled and hurled the knife. I shut my eyes for a second.

When I looked again, I saw a blade glittering over my head, spinning through the air. The littlest Louies were pawing at another goldfish on the guy's pants. They had thrown the kidnapper off balance when he hurled his knife.

The guy was running toward me again. I twisted away. He was right behind me, the needles crunching beneath his boots. I knew that this time he and Aunt Verona were not going to give up.

As I raced along, I saw the knife gleaming dully in the grass ahead of me. I snatched it up on the run. I didn't want this guy taking aim at me a second time.

The ground grew steeper. The forest was curving uphill. Was I racing toward the cliffs? I couldn't tell. I was running farther and farther away from Impact and from help. The pine trees gave way to bushes and shrubs. The ground grew so steep that I was practically climbing uphill. I grabbed at branches to help pull me along. Without realizing it, I had reached the crest of a hill. Above the pine forest, above the thick under-growth, now I could see the entire rock wall of Meteor International Park surrounding me, a gigantic wall of gray stone with dark grooves running up and down the steep sides like a petrified waterfall. I was on a high hill at the center of the park. A small lake shim-mered in the sun about twenty feet away. A white church steeple poked like a knife through the trees, somewhere beyond the water.

The kidnappers appeared over the edge of the hill. I heard Aunt Verona yell, "Antonio. There he is!"

Antonio! The name of the guy who had worked for my parents down in Agualar. The guy that Dad had written about in his journal, who had simply vanished one day. Vanished, like Aunt Verona had drowned.

The droning sound returned. I looked up and saw the twin helicopters zooming back toward the hill. An-tonio and Aunt Verona looked up, too. If only they hadn't messed up my smoke signals. How was I to get their attention? I didn't have time to make another fire.

The lake lay ahead of me. There was nowhere else to run.

I was afraid to look behind. Afraid I might slow down. I kept running toward the lake. The humming grew louder. Fiercer. It wasn't the helicopters this time. I saw the end of the lake formed a waterfall that fell down a sharp cliff in the hill. At the bottom of the falls sat the town of Impact. How was I going to get down there? If I ran into the lake, the force of the current might pull me over the falls.

I ran. Without thinking I ran toward the falls. I heard Antonio breathing hard behind me. I heard the sound of keys jingling at his belt.

Ahead, level with the top of the hill, where the falls began, a series of rocks stuck out from the white, gushing water. The rocks stood like rough stepping stones above the torrent. Could I cross them to safety? I would have to. It was either the rocks, the lake, or the waterfall.

I thought of Uncle Stoppard falling off the roof and into the lilac bush. I thought of the Blackfoot kid who almost fell off a mountain in the Rockies. I thought of my mother and father weeping over the body of some unknown woman they had believed was their sister and friend. I thought of poor Pablo, stabbed in the back because he was in the wrong place at the wrong time. And his friend Larry, waiting for his underwear to dry in the basement.

I looked at the first craggy rock that stood above the falls. It was at least seven feet from the shore. I forced every atom of energy in my body to the soles of my feet. In my right hand I squeezed Dad's lucky knife.

Give me luck, Dad, I thought. I need you.

All I could feel was air. Cold, rushing air.

The side of my head struck the rock. I had made the jump. My head felt strangely warm. When I put my hand to my face there was sticky blood on my fingers.

I looked across the rushing seven-foot swirl of water. Antonio and Aunt Verona stood on the other side. She was gesturing for him to jump after me, but he shook his head. She began hitting him in the head and shoulders. Antonio ignored her.

I shouted over the roaring of the falls. "Why did you take my picture? That wasn't gold! That belonged to me."

Aunt Verona looked at me. "Because, you fool, that is the only picture ever taken of the Horizontal Man. Without that picture, there is no proof that it ever really existed." She quickly glanced up, fear in her eyes. The helicopters had returned to the far side of the crater. If only they could see me, I thought.

Wait. I had the hunting knife clenched in my hand. The sun was almost directly overhead. I held the blade in front of me and jiggled it back and forth, hoping that its reflected light would attract the attention of the copters.

One of the copters paused on its flight across the crater. It grew smaller, and at first I thought it was zooming away from the falls. No, it was flying straight toward me. A guy in a helmet waved to me from the side of the copter. I waved back. I saw him buckle on a harness. He was lowering himself on a wire. He was going to rescue me!

Then I saw Aunt Verona do an odd thing. She pushed Antonio away from her and walked back from the edge of the lake. She stood staring at me, staring at the rocks. Measuring the distance. I could see her taking deep breaths. She was psyching herself up for the jump.

The guy on the wire was only twelve feet away. His feet dangled above me.

Aunt Verona started running.

She could reach me before the copter guy did. What then? Push me into the water? I would end up at the bottom of the falls like the poor Agualaran woman who was forced to take Aunt Verona's place in the doomed canoe.

The knife was still in my hand. I could use it for protection. I could throw it at Aunt Verona, slow her down, wound her. Instead, I held the blade in front of me again and jiggled it, just as I had for the helicopter. Maybe the reflected sunlight would blind Aunt Verona. Keep her from trying to jump.

I heard a loud scream. I realized it was coming from me. Aunt Verona grew smaller and smaller as her body twisted in the air, falling like a meteor toward the bottom of the falls.

I buried my face into the chest of the copter guy who stood next to me on the rock. He folded his arms around me.

It was a good thing the water sprayed all over us. All over my face.

I didn't want the copter guy to see that I was crying.

12
Lemon Aid

"I love waffles," said Jared. "How about waffles with raisins?"

"Don't joke," said Uncle Stoppard.

"I know we can't have a dog," I said, "but could we get a cat?"

"No animals allowed in the building," said Uncle Stoppard. "You know that."

"Rats are animals," I said.

Uncle Stoppard pulled the waffle maker plug from its socket, folded his arms, and stood leaning against the kitchen counter. "Do you want to eat breakfast or not?"

Jared laughed.

We were sitting in our kitchen eating, then *not* eating, breakfast. Uncle Stoppard had just tossed our raisin muffins. It was four days since I had been rescued from the waterfall above the town of Impact, Minnesota. A week and a half ago since we first saw Larry's horizontal body in the storage room. This morning, Jared came over to give us more news about the case. It was cool to watch a real live cop, in uniform, eat a waffle in your apartment. His blue cap and police belt hung over the back of his chair.

"Fish are pets, too," I suggested.

"Mr. Barrymore's fish were not pets," said Uncle Stoppard. "They were part of his work." Uncle Stoppard and I found out from Joan and Alison that Mr. Barrymore worked for a pet-cloning company called Animal Preserve. I had seen their commercials on TV. People could clone their favorite pets every few years and keep them around forever. So far the Animal Preserve scientists were successful with their dog and cat cloning programs (Doggy Ditto and RepliCat). Mr. Barrymore was working on their newest project, cloning fish. Each of the hundred goldfish in his apartment were actually the same one. I thought up a name for his new line: Fin Again.

Since all hundred fish were really, technically, the same one, I wondered if that meant somehow, technically, the eight fish that had given their lives to save me in the Grand Meteor Forest weren't really dead. Technically.

Can you clone parents?

"So how long did Verona and her pal live next door?" asked Uncle Stoppard.

"About a month. It was just like you figured. Verona saw your picture on the back cover of *Cold Feet* and knew where to find you. But how did you know about Verona seeing the photo, Stoppard? Antonio just confessed last night at the police station."

"Like I told Finn the day he got back from the park. It was the X ray from the hospital that gave me the idea."

"Uncle Stop is going to have an X ray of his head for his next book," I said.

"Yeah?" said Jared.

"I started thinking about my first author photo. The one that Finn took of me," said Uncle Stoppard. "Then I realized that was my *first* photo. Until then, no one knew what Stoppard Sterling looked like. And no one knew that Stoppard Sterling was really Stoppard Bumpelmeyer."

Jared almost spit out a hunk of waffle.

"It happens to be a very aristocratic German name. Anyway," Uncle Stoppard continued, "no one knew that Bumplemeyer had any connection with Sterling. Someone seeing that photo would know who I was. And where I lived. If that same someone was after the Agualaran gold, and knew about the Zwakes, I was the missing key to the treasure."

"And you figured only Verona Zwake fit that description?" asked Jared.

Uncle Stoppard nodded. "Only Leo, Anna, and Verona knew about me. And Verona figured I was the only link between her and the gold."

"But you still needed proof," said Jared.

And the kind of proof on Uncle Stoppard's brain these days was, of course, fingerprints. Several days ago when Jared had come by, Uncle Stoppard told Jared about his theory. Then, on the same day I was busy talking with our neighbors in the building and setting my trap, Jared dusted my dresser for fingerprints. Uncle Stoppard knew that the burglar was clever enough to always wear gloves. But then he thought about my missing coin. To pick up that thin piece of gold, you could not wear gloves. And you couldn't simply wipe the coin off the dresser, because a little wooden rail runs all around the top. That was the one place, Uncle Stoppard figured, where the burglar may have taken off his or her gloves. He was right. Jared found prints other than mine, and the next day he traced them to Aunt Verona.

"How did you identify Aunt Verona's fingerprints?" I asked Jared. "She never went to jail."

"No, but she was in the Army once."

"The Army takes fingerprints?" I said.

"I had my prints taken when I worked at a bank," said Uncle Stoppard. "Lots of other occupations require fingerprints."

"Didn't you think Aunt Verona was dead?" I said.

"Yes, but I was brainstorming. And you know how our family likes to think about dead things, Finn."

The image of Aunt Verona falling toward Impact, her thin arms flailing helplessly, made me want to give up thinking about dead things for quite a while.

"Are you okay, dude?" said Jared.

"I'm fine," I said.

"More waffles?" asked Uncle Stoppard. He put a hand on my shoulder.

"No, really, I'm fine."

"Why didn't you think some burglar simply got lucky and accidentally found the gold?" Jared asked Uncle Stoppard.

"Burglars usually take electronic items," said Uncle Stoppard. "Like TVs or stereos. Stuff they can sell for cash. But nothing like that was ever taken. Only the gold. In our storage room, Pablo kept a stereo set, but it wasn't stolen. And the other storage rooms were never disturbed. Not even the ones with padlocks rustier than ours, or no padlocks at all. It appeared as if we were the only targets."

"Alison's bike was stolen," I said.

No, that's right. It hadn't really been stolen.

After being rescued by the copter guy, the police were contacted and they called Uncle Stoppard. He and Jared rode up to Impact to bring me home. Then, while we drove back to Minneapolis in Jared's squad car, Uncle Stoppard told me everything. Including about the bike.

It was Mr. Barrymore who saw me being kidnapped. While hiding behind the garage from Alison and Joan, he saw two figures, a man and a woman, drag me to their car. He rushed into our apartment—Joan and Alison almost beat him up—and he told them to call 911. He explained about the kidnapping. Joan started to cry. She confessed to Uncle Stoppard that Alison had taken advantage of the fact that a thief was breaking into the building. Alison stole her own bike that night and hid it, Joan said, blaming it on our burglar. That way Alison could collect the insurance money. (Though the nurses *had* been nervous about a real thief skulking around the building. Jared guessed that Joan or Alison might have noticed the back door left unlocked after one of Aunt Verona's nightly scouting expeditions, or heard her creeping around the basement, before she and Antonio actually started stealing stuff.)

Alison was the person that Mr. Barrymore meant when he said, "She's lying." He saw Alison sneak her bike into her apartment. The night I was kidnapped, Mr. Barrymore knocked on Ms. Pryce's door and told her the truth. Ms. Pryce blew up. She ran all the way to the second floor to confront Alison. Mr. Barrymore ran outside and hid in the bushes. I guess he doesn't like confontations.

When Mr. Barrymore rushed in after I was kidnapped, Joan confessed to Uncle Stoppard because she wanted to help me. She didn't want the police confused by fake evidence. When the police arrived, Mr. Barrymore told them about the car. He watched the kidnappers' car squeal away, but wasn't able to remember the license plate numbers. Only the make and model of the car. He did remember something odd about the license, though. He said there was a bright red blot between the numbers and letters on the plate. The police realized he had seen a Texas plate. Those particular plates have a small, but bright red, Texas-shaped figure smack in the center. (Just as Minnesota plates have blue Minnesota-shaped figures in their centers.) The only plates in the whole country that have something red in the center are from Texas. When the police questioned our neighbors, they discovered that a married couple from Texas lived next door. That's how they were able to trace the car and find out who owned it.

And when Uncle Stoppard received a phone call from the kidnappers—demanding the golden spoon in exchange for my safety—the police traced the call to a small town outside of Minneapolis. The police then realized the kidnappers were heading north instead of south, hoping to slip across the Canadian border.

"It's weird how we never noticed them living next door," I said.

"How many people really know their neighbors?" said Jared.

"Or their relatives," added Uncle Stoppard.

My next question I wasn't sure if I wanted answered. "Did she kill Larry?"

Jared gulped down an entire glass of orange juice, wiped his mouth on a napkin, then stared at me. "No, kid, she didn't. Morado confessed killing him." Over a third helping of waffles, Jared further explained that Antonio Morado and Verona (they got married in Mexico) had moved in next door in order to keep an eye on us. It was Verona who picked the locks of our apartment building to get into the storage room.

"I guess when you're an archeologist used to breaking into ancient temples and sealed tombs, a modern-day padlock is no problem," Jared said.

Pablo's friend Larry had been in the basement washing clothes last Friday night, just as Uncle Stoppard guessed. Larry noticed Antonio and Verona in the storage room quietly removing our gold. Poor Larry didn't know who they were. He thought they lived in the building. He walked over to chat with them, and Antonio killed him by bashing in his head with the Horizontal Man. Antonio was afraid of being identified in case the police should ever question Larry about the break-in.

Verona panicked.

She took one look at Larry stretched out on the floor and fled through the basement window. She didn't use the backdoor because she was afraid someone might come down the stairs looking for Larry. That was why Uncle Stoppard and I couldn't find any signs of a break-in around the window. No one broke *in*. They broke *out*. Antonio climbed out the window after he dragged Larry inside the storage room and padlocked the door.

And if only poor Larry hadn't been eating cheese-flavored chips while he was doing his laundry that night. (Jared had shared that bit of info, too.)

The two crooks waited a few days to see if the body would be discovered. Since the police never came to the apartment building, they figured they were safe. Antonio talked Verona into going back and recovering the Horizontal Man. On Sunday, she slipped back in through the basement window, partially hidden by the lilac bushes, picked up the Horizontal Man, and tried washing off the blood in one of the washtubs. While she was down there, Verona gathered up a few more gold artifacts, including the spoon. The statue was too heavy and awkward to carry out the window so she waited until things seemed quiet and then walked up the basement stairs.

"She sure had guts," I said.

"And muscles," said Jared. "That statue weighs over seventy-five pounds."

"That's as much as a King Louie!" I said.

"She must have figured she'd attract less attention walking out the back door of a building than if she climbed through a window in broad daylight," said Uncle Stoppard.

When Aunt Verona trudged up the back stairs on Sunday with her ton of gold, she heard someone at the back entrance, someone coming in from outside. She tried Pablo's door, which was directly across from the stairs, and hid inside. Since the apartment was empty, she stayed there a moment to catch her breath (this was what Antonio confessed, according to Jared).

"Why was Pablo's door unlocked?" I asked.

"It was still unlocked from when Larry went downstairs to do his laundry two days earlier," said Jared.

"But Verona could have easily picked it, if she needed to, like she did with the other locks."

While sitting in Pablo's kitchen, Aunt Verona noticed blood on the gold spoon. She washed some of it off in Pablo's sink and set the spoon in the dish rack. Then she walked around the apartment with the Horizontal Man, looking for a bag or box to carry it in. She heard someone at the front door. It was me and Ms. Pryce! Verona put the gold statue down on Pablo's coffee table, and then hid in a closet.

"Aunt Verona, Ms. Pryce, and me were in Pablo's apartment at the same time?" I asked.

"As soon as you and Ms. Pryce left Pablo's apartment," said Jared, "she picked up the statue, waited a few minutes, then walked out the back and slipped into her apartment next door as if she was out for a Sunday walk."

"She forgot the spoon," said Uncle Stoppard.

"It was Verona's greed for the spoon that made her risk coming back to the basement while you were here in your apartment," said Jared. "That's when she attacked Pablo in the basement with the ski pole. It was the same kind of situation as with Larry. Verona was surprised to find Pablo in the storage locker ahead of her, and didn't want him turning around to see her. Luckily, Pablo's wounds weren't fatal."

"And luckily they didn't try looking for the spoon up here," I said. "Or else I wouldn't have been able to set up my trap."

"If you hadn't set that dangerous trap," said Uncle Stoppard, "you wouldn't have been kidnapped."

"But Aunt Verona and Antonio might have decided to leave Minneapolis early unless I had tempted them with the golden spoon." They must have overheard me talking to Ms. Pryce when she was sweeping the sidewalk. It was creepy knowing that Aunt Verona had lived only a few yards away from us. And every day she was spying on us.

"But what if Barrymore hadn't seen the car?" said Uncle Stoppard. "The cops wouldn't have been able to trace the owners, alert the border patrol, send out officers looking for you—"

"See?" I said. "My trap worked."

Jared looked at Uncle Stoppard. "Sure did, buddy," Jared said to me.

Uncle Stoppard blew his nose. "More waffles?" he asked.

We all had enough.

"When do those Ackerberg Institute people come pick up the gold?" asked Jared.

"Middle of the week," said Uncle Stoppard. He was careful to avoid looking at me when he said this. The Horizontal Man, the golden spoon, and the other artifacts would be living with us for only a few more days. Among the stolen items recovered by the police, the only one that officially belonged to me was the photo of my parents in Agualar.

Did I really want that Maya stuff hanging around? I remembered how angry I had been with Pablo when I thought he had stolen *my* golden spoon. Larry was dead because Antonio thought the gold belonged to *him*. Maybe the Zwake Curse would vanish as soon as the treasure was shipped off to the museum. I guess I had my treasure. It was sitting inside its frame on top of my dresser.

"Looks like a beautiful day," said Uncle Stoppard. "Finn, let's you and I head over to Cafe Olé."

Cafe Olé? Mariachi music? Cactus plants?

"I think I've had enough southern stuff for a while," I said.

"Really?" asked Uncle Stoppard. He had a funny gleam in his cucumber eyes.

"That rules out the Drinkin' Incan," said Jared.

"Let's go somewhere new."

"Good idea," said Uncle Stoppard. "How would you like to go to Agualar?"

A Note from Stoppard Sterling

Raccoons are not, strictly speaking, rodents. They are members of the *Carnivora* order of mammals, that is, they are meat-eaters with large canine teeth. Rats and mice, true members of the order *Rodentia,* do not possess canines. Finnegan did not have this distinction in mind when, being chased by the King Louis raccoons in Grand Meteor Forest, he said he hated all rodents, no matter what their size. To him, a rodent was any beady-eyed mammal that scooted across the ground, ready to chomp on anything that moved. With this definition in mind, and considering the teeth marks on the Horizontal Man of Agualar, I would venture to say that Finnegan himself was once a rodent. When I mentioned this to him, he did not find it amusing.

Most raccoons are shy of human contact. But the scent of their favorite food—in this case, fish—will make a hungry creature do extraordinary things.

I also pointed out to my nephew how fortunate he was to extricate himself from the trunk of Mr. Morado's car. Not every trunk can be opened so easily, as I discovered from reading Philip Weiss's informative essay, "How to Get Out of a Locked Trunk." I would certainly advise no one to attempt this stunt without professional supervision, and definitely not in the presence of kidnappers or formerly dead relatives.

FINNEGAN ZWAKE

COMING SOON!

THE NEXT
FINNEGAN ZWAKE MYSTERY

THIRTEEN-YEAR-OLD FINNEGAN ZWAKE, HIS UNCLE STOPPARD, A BESTSELLING MYSTERY WRITER, AND THEIR FRIEND JARED ARE OFF TO AN ARCHAEOLOGICAL DIG IN SUNNY AGUALAR, LAND OF GIANT CACTI, JUNGLES, AND DINOSAURS. DEAD ONES, THAT IS.

WHILE FINN AND HIS UNCLE ARE DIGGING UP TREASURE, THE CREW IS DIGGING UP VERY VALUABLE DINOSAUR EGGS. BUT DIGGING TOO DEEPLY CAN STIR UP TROUBLE, NOT TO MENTION A MURDER, OR TWO, OR THREE....

READ

THE WORM TUNNEL

By Michael Dahl

An Archway Paperback
Published by Pocket Books

2133